"Jo, My Darling, You're like a Fire in My Blood."

Roarke's remark triggered a primitive reflex in the pit of her stomach. She wanted to tell him that she felt the same way, but she couldn't speak. However, her trembling body revealed to Roarke that his desires were matched.

He responded by kissing her more and more intensely, and the fire within Jo blazed through every fiber of her body.

Soon they were sprawled across her bed, their bodies entwined in a passionate embrace.

Jo lost all sense of time and place. For the moment, Roarke was the only thing that existed in her universe. More than anything else, Jo wanted to please him. . . .

LINDA SUNSHINE

has been both an editor and author, and says she loves working on books—from any angle. She left publishing to devote herself full time to her first interest, writing. Other interests include ballet and horseback riding.

Dear Reader:

SILHOUETTE DESIRE is an exciting new line of contemporary romances from Silhouette Books. During the past year, many Silhouette readers have written in telling us what other types of stories they'd like to read from Silhouette, and we've kept these comments and suggestions in mind in developing SILHOUETTE DESIRE.

DESIREs feature all of the elements you like to see in a romance, plus a more sensual, provocative story. So if you want to experience all the excitement, passion and joy of falling in love, then SILHOUETTE DESIRE is for you.

I hope you enjoy this book and all the wonderful stories to come from SILHOUETTE DESIRE. I'd appreciate any thoughts you'd like to share with us on new SILHOUETTE DESIRE, and I invite you to write to us at the address below:

Karen Solem
Editor-in-Chief
Silhouette Books
P.O. Box 769
New York, N.Y. 10019

LINDA SUNSHINE
Constant Stranger

Silhouette Desire

Published by Silhouette Books New York

America's Publisher of Contemporary Romance

SILHOUETTE BOOKS, a Simon & Schuster Division of
GULF & WESTERN CORPORATION
1230 Avenue of the Americas, New York, N.Y. 10020

ISBN: 0-671-45129-4

First Silhouette Books printing October, 1982

10 9 8 7 6 5 4 3 2 1

Constant Stranger

1

Never believe anything you hear at an employment agency. Joanna Davenport could swear that every agency in New York City was staffed by total incompetents who cheerfully sent applicants like herself on wild-goose chases. Today was Jo's seventh job interview in two weeks. Three times she'd been sent for jobs that didn't exist and twice for positions that had been filled before Jo was even interviewed. Unfortunately, Jo couldn't give up, she desperately needed a job.

So, Jo took a deep breath and circled her way through the revolving doors of the huge glass skyscraper on Sixth Avenue. Today's interview was for a secretarial job at a publishing company. Although it sounded terrific, by now Jo had learned to keep her optimism in check.

Jo quickly found the listing for Harris House Publishers on the big board in the lobby. The company was located on the twentieth floor and Jo took the floor number as a good omen.

Joanna's twentieth birthday was tomorrow and, somehow, seeing the number 20 on the board gave her the encouragement she needed at the moment. From her mother, Jo had inherited a strange brand of superstition; she looked for good omens in everyday occurrences.

When the elevator doors slid open on the twentieth floor, Joanna was startled by the sight of herself in the huge floor-to-ceiling mirror on the wall facing her. She hardly recognized her reflection.

There in the mirror was the image of a petite junior executive. Her long golden hair was tightly braided and wrapped around her head. Her black cloth coat, kid pumps, and attaché case gave her a look of efficiency and practicality. It's too severe, she thought to herself; I look like I'm on my way to a funeral. Nervously, Jo tried to fix the loose strands of hair that had fallen down her neck. Then she turned to the receptionist who was sitting behind a huge white formica desk in the reception area.

"I'm here to see Mrs. Janet Tarlin," Jo said as she fumbled in her purse, finally extracting a small piece of pink paper. "See." She unfolded the paper and gave it to the woman. "The Avery Employment Agency sent me over."

The woman glanced at the pink slip. "Okay. Why don't you have a seat and I'll tell Janet, um . . . Mrs. Tarlin, you're here."

Jo smiled as the woman informed Mrs. Tarlin's office that someone was waiting to see her. She returned the phone to its cradle. "Mrs. Tarlin is in conference at the moment but her assistant said she'll be able to see you in

a few minutes. You can hang your coat in this closet."
The woman pointed to a door behind her desk.

Jo crossed the room and hung her coat in the small
closet. She had to pass the mirror again to get back to the
couch. She tried not to stare at her reflection but it was
impossible. At least my suit is a bit more cheerful than my
coat, she thought to herself.

Jo had bought the pale green gabardine suit and ivory
silk blouse two weeks before arriving in New York. In the
past month, she had worn it to every one of her
interviews.

When she wasn't wearing the suit, Jo had on faded
jeans and a sweat shirt which she wore whenever she
went out looking for a cheap apartment. She hadn't been
lucky in either outfit. She was still living in an uptown
"hotel for women" (really a boarding house) and, as yet,
she hadn't come close to landing an office job. Her
savings were running low and, if she didn't find a job
soon, she'd have to settle for waitressing or something
equally unpleasant. Joanna simply couldn't go back to
Vermont now.

Jo had graduated from high school in Falls Creek a
year and a half ago. Since then she'd worked in a small
advertising agency near home. She'd been lucky to get
the work in a small town like Falls Creek. But, unfortunately, the office had folded and Jo had been out of a
good job.

Meanwhile, Jo's mother had come to depend on her
daughter's paycheck to help make ends meet after Jo's
dad died three years ago. Jo had been scared to leave
Falls Creek, but New York City was the only answer if she
wanted to continue supporting herself and helping her
mother.

At first the noise and confusion of the big city had rattled Jo's nerves. Gradually, though, she began to get used to it and her life settled into a dull routine of job interviews and apartment hunting. But she felt lonely and unsettled in the city. The girls at her hotel were nice enough, but everyone was always rushing around. No one settled in one place long enough to start a conversation, much less a friendship.

Jo pushed aside thoughts of her current problems. She wanted to be in a cheerful frame of mind in order to make a good impression on Mrs. Tarlin. She reached over and grabbed a magazine from the coffee table in front of her. She started scanning it before she realized that it wasn't a magazine at all. The front cover read "Harris House, Spring Catalog." On each page was a picture of a book jacket and a few paragraphs describing the contents of each book.

Jo had always been an avid reader; she recognized several of the authors among the prestigious listing of titles. Harris House published her favorite writer, Murphy Roarke, and she noticed that a new Roarke title was due to be published in a few months. She took the sight of Roarke's familiar name as another good omen.

When she finished reading about the last title in the catalog, an encyclopedia of dogs, she glanced down at her watch and shifted nervously on the couch. Joanna had been waiting for over an hour. So much for lucky omens, she thought to herself. This is just another wild-goose chase. Obviously, Mrs. Tarlin's forgotten all about me and I've got to come up with a graceful exit in front of this nice receptionist.

Jo got up off the couch, smoothing down the wrinkles

in her skirt, and started to cross the room. Before she got to the closet, however, a door leading to the inner offices swung open and a man came rushing out. Not looking where he was going, he crashed into Jo. She was caught completely off balance. He hit her left shoulder so hard that she spun around and stumbled backwards. Her purse went flying across the room, spilling its contents on the pale carpeting.

It had all happened so quickly that Jo was slightly dazed when she felt a hand grab her arm and break her fall.

"Damn! I'm sorry, miss. You okay?"

Jo turned her head toward the husky male voice. Towering above her was the most handsome face she'd ever seen. His deep-set eyes were coal black. His brown hair gleamed with streaks of copper, and the contrast highlighted his ruddy complexion. It flashed through Jo's mind that he must be a model for one of the book jackets she'd just seen in the Harris House catalog.

"Are you all right?" he repeated. Although his voice was full of concern, his eyes swept over Jo's trim figure. She could feel the rush of color to her cheeks. Her jade eyes clouded over.

With her free hand she self-consciously tugged at the hemline of her skirt but he continued to stare admiringly at her long legs.

Standing directly behind him was a slender, attractive woman in her late thirties or early forties. "Murphy!" she cried. "What have you done to this poor woman?"

"It's okay, I'm fine," Jo stammered. "Really . . . I'm okay." She reached over to retrieve the contents of her purse.

"Here," he said, bending down towards her. "Let me at least help you with that."

The woman also bent down to help. "Really, Murphy, if you weren't in such a snit over that last set of corrections this would never have happened. You must learn to control that temper of yours." She spoke sternly but with great affection, like a mother reprimanding her favorite child.

The tall stranger pointed at her. "I'll control my temper when you control your blue pencil, Janet." He turned to Jo. "Wouldn't *you* be upset if your best chapter was just cut to shreds for no apparent reason?" he asked.

Jo shrugged helplessly, not knowing what to make of the question.

"Anyway, I'm part Irish and I do have one hell of a temper," he added as if that explained everything. "But I'm sorry I took it out on you.

"Although," he continued, "if I had to knock someone over, I certainly couldn't have chosen a more beautiful opponent."

He grinned from ear to ear and his expression was charmingly boyish.

Jo's first instinct was to return the smile but she immediately suppressed the urge. He's too handsome for his own good, she thought contemptuously to herself.

Quickly, she stuffed her purse with her belongings.

He stood up first and extended his hand towards her. She hesitated a moment before placing her hand in his. Effortlessly, he pulled her to a standing position.

He held her at arm's length and whisked the back of his hand across her shoulders and down her sleeves, brushing lint from her jacket. She shivered at the lightness of his touch.

"You okay now?" he asked. Apparently, he wasn't aware of the effect he was having on Jo.

She nodded slowly.

He smiled once more, turned on his heel and strode over to the elevator which was just opening.

At the elevator he turned and waved at Jo before he disappeared behind the closing doors.

Jo and the woman he had called Janet stood staring after him. Jo could still feel the stranger's hands on her as she unconsciously stroked her arm.

At the same moment, both women turned to each other.

"Forgive him," the woman said to Jo. "He's a famous *author*, you know." She emphasized the word "author" as if it were a disease.

Jo blinked twice. She shivered again as she remembered the sensation of the tall stranger's coal-black eyes sweeping over her body. The memory of his face towering above her was burned into her vision like a red spot from a flashing lightbulb.

Meanwhile, the woman turned and started back towards the offices.

"Mrs. Tarlin," the receptionist called out, "this is the young woman who's been waiting for you all morning."

A look of horror spread slowly over Janet Tarlin's face. "Oh dear, I'd forgotten all about you. You're here for the secretarial job, aren't you?"

Jo nodded as the older woman retraced her steps back to Jo's side. "Forgive me, my dear. First I keep you waiting all this time and then my author practically knocks you out. I'm terribly sorry about all this."

"It's okay," Jo said politely. "Maybe I should come back when you're not so busy."

"Absolutely not. You come into my office. The least I can do is talk to you right now." She grabbed Jo's arm and led her through the door. Jo glanced back at the receptionist and smiled appreciatively at her.

Jo was led through a winding corridor. On her left were rows of offices, many with open doors. On her right was an open area of desks where a dozen young women sat typing or talking on the phone.

At the end of the corridor, Mrs. Tarlin led Jo into a corner office. The room was a complete shambles. Books and magazines were scattered everywhere. Overflowing manuscripts threatened to topple off every available tabletop. The walls were covered with book jackets, scraps of paper scrawled with notes, and a huge oaktag chart. On a shelf under the window were several glass-framed photographs of children. In spite of all the clutter, the room had a cozy, hardworking feel to it.

Janet moved behind a large wooden desk loaded with papers, folders and books. She indicated that Jo should take a seat opposite the desk.

"Now then," Janet said, "let's talk about you. Did you bring along your résumé?"

"Yes, of course." Jo reached into her attaché case and extracted a piece of paper. Nervously, she handed the résumé to Mrs. Tarlin. As always, Jo felt uncomfortable handing over her résumé. It seemed like such an insubstantial piece of paper to her. She was certain that everyone else's résumé was longer and much more exciting than her own.

Janet reached into a pile of papers on her desk, pulled out a pair of tortoiseshell glasses and perched them precariously on the bridge of her nose. "Let's see here." She quickly scanned the résumé. "I see your last job was

14

with the Ridgeway Advertising Agency in Falls Creek, Vermont. What did you do there?"

"A little bit of everything really. I can type about 60 words per minute and take dictation. Of course I handled the correspondence and the phones. Sometimes I even got to write some of the copy; that was the really interesting part of the job."

"Oh!" Janet exclaimed, her eyebrows lifting when Jo mentioned the writing part of her last job. "Did you bring a sample of your writing?"

"Well, yes, I did. But I'm a little reluctant to show it to you." Jo extracted a small brochure from her case and pointed it toward Janet. "It's only a paint catalog and it's not very interesting."

"Just hand it over," Janet said, reaching across the desk for the brochure. "Catalog copy is catalog copy. Selling paint isn't all that different from selling books."

Jo was shocked that Janet would compare selling paint to selling books. After all, books were works of art and paint was, well, only paint.

"This is excellent copy," Janet said as she scanned the brochure. "The descriptions are crisp and to the point." She nodded approvingly.

Jo was delighted by the compliment. "Thank you, Mrs. Tarlin." She smiled gratefully. "That's the first encouraging thing I've heard in a long time."

"Job hunting isn't much fun, is it?" Janet asked sympathetically.

"Frankly, no. And I'm getting very discouraged. I thought once I got to New York, there would be lots of job opportunities. But it seems that there's not much more here than there was in Falls Creek."

"Now, you mustn't get disheartened. You just have to

keep plugging away at it." Janet leaned back in her chair. "I remember when I was looking for my first job in New York. Oh, this was many years ago, more years than I care to remember. My husband and I had just moved to the city—"

Before Janet could continue, her office door flew open and in rushed the stranger who'd collided into Jo only a few minutes ago. Jo wondered if he ever entered a room at a normal pace.

"Janet, I'm sorry to interrupt you," he said hastily. "But this is an emergency. Did I leave my wallet here? I got all the way to the subway before I realized that . . ." He stopped his rush of words when he noticed Jo sitting opposite Janet's chair. His black eyes squinted in delight.

"Well, hello again." He smiled at Jo. "Didn't mean to barge in on you. I'll have to apologize once more." He shook his head. "Two apologies and we haven't met yet." He glanced at Janet.

Janet sighed. "Murphy Roarke, may I introduce Joanna Davenport?"

"You're Murphy Roarke?" Jo's eyes widened in disbelief.

He laughed deeply. "You're Joanna Davenport?" He imitated the disbelief in her voice.

She could feel her cheeks flush. She was embarrassed but excited to be talking to one of her favorite authors. "Jo Davenport," she said. "Please call me Jo."

"Jo." He nodded as if he liked the sound of it. "What're you here for, Jo? Trying to peddle your latest novel to Janet? I warn you, as an editor, she's a true slave driver." He leaned against Janet's desk as if he had all the time in the world to chat with Jo.

"Novel? Oh no, I . . ."

"Ah ha! Non-fiction writer, then? Let me guess." He stroked his chin thoughtfully. "You've written a biography of . . . Virginia Woolf. No, no. Hemingway. You're definitely the Hemingway type. Intelligent, direct and"—his eyes swept down to her slender ankles—"compact."

His good-natured tone confused Jo. She squirmed uncomfortably in her chair. Was he mocking her, flirting with her, or just being an eccentric "famous author" as Janet Tarlin had previously warned?

"Actually, I'm here for a job interview," Jo replied with as much sophistication as she could muster. "And if I were to write a biography, it wouldn't be of Ernest Hemingway. Carlos Baker has more than sufficiently covered Hemingway's life."

Murphy crossed his arms over his chest and nodded several times, impressed with her response. "Touché! And very true. Very true indeed," he said.

Jo grinned, feeling a little more self-confident.

Murphy warmly returned her smile. "Are you living in the city?" he asked.

"I'm trying to. Apartments are awfully hard to come by in New York," Jo said. Then, from the corner of her eye, Jo caught sight of Mrs. Tarlin. A hard look of annoyance had settled on her face.

"This is all very interesting," Janet Tarlin said, her voice raised slightly. "But we are in the middle of an interview, Murphy. If you don't mind, of course. I believe *I* should be the one asking the questions."

Murphy shrugged his shoulders and waved his hand at Janet. "Of course," he said as he walked behind Jo's chair to the couch at the far end of the office. He reached

17

behind the cushions and pulled out a worn wallet. "Yes, I thought it must've fallen out back there." He winked knowingly at Janet who seemed embarrassed by his gesture.

Murphy stuffed his wallet into the back pocket of his faded jeans and walked to the door of the office. "Well, I'm glad to learn you're not a writer. Authors absolutely detest competition." He turned to Janet. "My advice to you, Janet, is to hire this young woman immediately. Anyone who knows her Hemingway would be a real asset in this place." He stared at Jo but she looked away, strangely agitated by the intensity of his gaze.

"Good luck, Jo. I hope you find a job and an apartment real soon," he said before he left the office.

Janet pulled off her glasses and smiled at Jo. "So, that's our Mr. Roarke. What do you think of him?"

"Well, he isn't quite what I expected." Jo tried to sound diplomatic. "I mean, he's not at all like his writing."

Janet smiled. "I'm delighted to hear that you're familiar with Murphy's work. Tell me, what kind of man were you expecting?"

"Well, his writing is so precise. So well-organized. And, in person, he seems a little . . ." She groped for the correct word.

"I think 'unpredictable' might be an apt description," Janet interrupted. "But he's tremendously talented," she sighed. "And not bad-looking, either."

"No, not bad-looking," Jo said thoughtfully. "If you like that type, of course," she added hastily.

"Indeed." Janet smiled. "Well, I'm very impressed with this interview, not to mention your writing ability and your forbearance with Mr. Roarke. But I'm afraid I've got to send you on your way." Janet glanced at her watch. "I'm already ten minutes late for an advertising meeting."

Jo stood up quickly. "Of course," she said, trying to hide her disappointment. "Thank you for seeing me."

"It was my pleasure, Jo. Thank you for your patience."

Jo didn't know what else to say. Obviously, she hadn't gotten the job. She turned towards the door.

"Oh, by the way, dear. Is this your correct phone number?" Janet Tarlin was pointing to Jo's résumé.

"Yes," Jo replied hopefully. "I'm staying at that hotel until I find an apartment."

"Good. I have one more interview this afternoon. I'll call you later today and let you know my final decision. As of now, you're very high on my list of candidates."

Jo's face broke into a wide grin. Even if she didn't get the job, this was the most promising interview she'd had since arriving in New York. "Thank you again, Mrs. Tarlin. I'll look forward to hearing from you."

Janet escorted Jo to the reception area and patted her arm encouragingly before turning back into the offices.

Jo retrieved her coat and thanked the receptionist. Alone in the elevator, she thought about the events of the past hour, remembering with chagrin how awkwardly she had behaved in front of Roarke.

She continued to chide herself for her lack of sophistication during the subway ride which ended at her hotel. Hunger finally took her mind off her shortcomings, and before she went to her room, she stopped at the corner deli and bought a ham sandwich and an apple. She would much rather have chosen the plump pink shrimp marked $8.99 a pound, but she could barely afford the sandwich.

Back in her room, sitting alone on her bed, Jo ate her sandwich and apple and remembered the dreams she had had when she came to New York. She had been certain that a whole new life awaited her in New York, complete with an exciting career and a glamorous social life. In her fantasy about Manhattan, the glamorous life meant elegant French restaurants, Broadway shows, discotheques, and intimate midnight supper clubs with someone like Roarke.

None of these dreams had materialized, not yet at least. And, even worse, on the eve of her twentieth birthday, Jo was alone in a rundown hotel, waiting desperately for the phone to ring. She got more and more discouraged as the minutes passed into hours.

At 7:30, when she had given up hope, she heard the pay phone ringing in the hall outside her room. As always, it was answered immediately. The girls in her hotel paid serious attention to the telephone.

Jo jumped when she heard a heavy rapping on her door. "Joanna, phone call for you," someone yelled through the closed door.

Jo ran to the phone. "Hello," she said eagerly into the mouthpiece.

"Joanna, hi. It's Janet Tarlin."

"Yes, Mrs. Tarlin," Jo said breathlessly, crossing her fingers on both hands at the same time.

"Listen, Jo, my five-thirty interviewee was wearing a silver lamé tank top and torn jeans. Can you imagine?" Janet laughed.

Bless her disco heart, thought Jo to herself. "You're kidding," she said weakly.

"I kid you not, my dear. Soooo, if you're still interested, the job is yours."

Jo was too shocked to speak.

"Did you hear me, dear? I said the job was yours. Okay?"

"Yes, yes, that's better than okay. That's great. When do I start?"

Janet giggled on the other end of the phone. "Aren't you going to ask about the salary?"

Jo slapped her hand to her forehead. What a dolt she must think I am, she thought to herself. "Yes, I was just about to ask," she lied.

"The job pays two hundred a week, which I know is low with today's inflation, but that's what it is. Publishing is not known for its terrific salaries."

"Two hundred a week sounds fine to me," Jo said. In fact, any salary would seem fine with her dwindling checking account and, besides, two hundred dollars a week was almost double her Falls Creek salary.

"Okay, but I must warn you I'm an absolute tyrant to work for. The hours are endless and I'll have you typing your fingers to the bone. Murphy Roarke is an absolute angel compared to some of the authors you'll be working with. Are you sure you don't want to think about this overnight?"

"Absolutely not, it sounds perfect. When do I start?"

"That's the spirit!" Janet laughed. "All right, I'll see you tomorrow at nine o'clock sharp. Bye." The phone went dead.

Jo hung up the phone, spun around and clapped her hands together loudly. "I got it!" she yelled to no one in particular as she skipped into her room.

Picking up the Harris House catalog, Jo tore out the

page on Murphy Roarke and stuck it in the frame of her bureau mirror. Impulsively, she winked at the photo of Roarke before she climbed into bed later that night.

Feeling a little dizzy from the excitement of Janet's call, Jo fell asleep dreaming of lunchtime shopping sprees and midnight buggy rides through Central Park with a handsome copper-haired writer.

2

On the morning of her twentieth birthday, Joanna Davenport jumped out of bed at seven o'clock. She showered quickly. Standing before the foggy mirror, Jo carefully wrapped her long blond hair into a neat French knot. She dressed in her gray wool skirt and pale pink Victorian blouse. For extra luck, she pinned her mother's cameo brooch to her high collar.

She arrived at Harris House exactly at nine o'clock. The next thing she knew, Janet Tarlin sent her to the personnel department where Jo was instructed to fill out a stack of blank forms. Jo completed three of the forms in front of the Personnel Director and, in return, was given two more forms. By ten-thirty, Jo was sitting at a small desk in front of Mrs. Tarlin's office, finishing the last of the forms.

The form was for her Blue Cross medical coverage,

and she was instructed to check off all her childhood illnesses. Measles, yes. Mumps, yes. Chicken pox. Was it chicken pox or tonsillitis that had kept Jo from attending the fourth-grade picnic? She stared thoughtfully at the form, slowly chewing the end of her pencil.

Suddenly, like a flash of radar, her sixth sense picked up the presence of someone standing behind her. She turned her head. Towering over her right shoulder was Murphy Roarke. His eyes were scanning the medical form in front of her. Instinctively, her arm reached over to cover the half-completed form.

"Please continue," he said lightly. "Don't mind me. I'm a natural born snoop."

"It's not very polite to sneak up on a person," she retorted, turning over the form on her desk.

"Why not? How else could I have learned about your bouts of measles and mumps?" He grinned playfully, cocking an eyebrow at her.

Jo felt the same confusion in his presence that she'd felt yesterday. "I can't imagine why that's of any interest to you," she said defensively, hoping her agitation wasn't apparent to him.

"You'd be surprised what's interesting to me." He lowered his voice, bending his head to whisper in her ear. "Frankly, I find everything about you interesting." She could feel his warm breath on her neck.

Jo twirled the pencil in her hand. Roarke moved around to the front of her desk. His muscular thigh lightly brushed against her elbow. He didn't seem aware that he'd touched her, but Jo felt as though her arm had been singed. "So I see double congratulations are in order. First, let me congratulate you on your new job."

"Thank you," she replied, averting her eyes.

"And, let me be the first one today to wish you a happy birthday!"

"But . . . how did you know it's my birthday?" she stammered.

He pointed to the form on her desk. "It's the first thing Blue Cross wanted to know, after your full name. By the way, what does the 'E' stand for?"

"What 'E'?"

"Joanna *E.* Davenport. Your middle initial."

She laughed in spite of her nervousness. How long had he been standing there behind her? she wondered. "I think I'll keep that little secret to myself." She meant to sound sarcastic but the remark was thrown out like a challenge.

"Ah, good." Roarke rubbed his hands together. "I love secrets." He grinned. His arms were crossed over his chest and he was intently watching Jo.

The way he stared at her made Jo quite nervous but it was also strangely exciting. She tried telling herself that he was just like any other man, but she knew it wasn't true. I'd better fight fire with fire, she thought to herself. She straightened her shoulders defiantly. "Why are you staring at me?" she demanded.

The remark seemed to surprise him. "Was I staring?" He shrugged. "Sorry, but you're an extremely beautiful woman," he added simply.

He could see that his remark embarrassed her and, as if he wanted to make amends, he changed the subject. "Listen, Jo, could you do me a favor?" He held out a long, thin piece of paper. "Look at this galley for me, will you? I've tried to proofread it a dozen times but I can't see any mistakes, since I wrote the original copy myself.

"A messenger is coming to pick it up any minute. Janet and Dacey are tied up at the moment and I haven't got time to run down to Copyediting. Please?" His voice was all business but he smiled charmingly at her.

"Sure," Jo said, feeling more confident talking about business than about herself. She'd done some proofreading at her last job, so she knew the basic procedure.

Murphy handed the long galley to Jo. The copy concerned Roarke's new book, *The Finlandia Affair.*

Jo noticed one misspelled word, but that was the only mistake she could find in the copy.

As she started to hand the galley back to Roarke, she noticed an italicized footnote at the bottom of the copy. "Wait a minute," she said. "I didn't notice the footnote."

The footnote was brief. It read: *"Murphy Roarke is the esteemed author of two bestselling novels,* Journeys Inland *and* Safekeeping. *He is unmarried, lives in New York's Greenwich Village, and teaches Creative Writing at Columbia University."*

Jo smiled to herself as Roarke quickly grabbed at the galley, trying to get it before Jo could finish reading the footnote. "Hey! Not fair," he said.

Jo leaned back in her chair. "Don't mind me," she said with a wave of her hand. "I'm a natural born snoop."

They burst out laughing together.

"Thanks for reading this for me," he said, lifting the galley for a moment. "I appreciate it."

"You're welcome," Jo said. "I enjoyed it and I'm looking forward to reading *The Finlandia Affair.*"

"Good," he said with a smile. "In payment for your prompt editorial services, I'd like to buy you a drink tonight. How about it?"

The invitation came as a total shock to Jo. "Well, I don't know," she hedged, hoping to regain her composure. "It's only my first day here. I may have to work late."

"On your birthday? Nonsense. Come on, let's celebrate the occasion with a drink. Unless you have other plans . . ." His voice trailed off.

"No, I don't," Jo said quickly.

"Good, then it's settled." His smile was so inviting and Jo was so flattered by his warm attention that she found it impossible to refuse him.

"Well, okay," she said with a shy smile.

"Great!" He slapped his hand on her desk. "I'll be by here about six o'clock to pick you up." He turned and strode over to the empty office next to Mrs. Tarlin's. "Now I'll leave you to your forms. It's into the salt mines for me." He winked at her before disappearing into the office.

Jo stared at the closed door for a moment. Her pulse was racing. She had a date tonight with Murphy Roarke! Her girlfriends back home in Falls Creek would never believe it. She could hardly believe it herself. She shook her head and laughed quietly to herself. Were her fantasies going to materialize after all? With renewed vigor, she returned to the Blue Cross form. Yes, it had been chicken pox in the fourth grade, tonsillitis in the sixth grade.

About half an hour later, Jo heard Janet's voice calling her from behind the closed door to her corner office. "Jo, please come in here for a minute."

Jo opened Janet's door and entered the cluttered office. Janet gestured for Jo to sit on a small couch in the back of the office. Sitting in the visitor's chair opposite Janet's desk was a young woman with dark curly hair.

"Now, Joanna, are you all squared away with Personnel?"

"I think so," Jo replied. "My desk is covered with forms to fill out, but I think I'm officially employed at Harris House by now. I can't figure out why they need half the information they requested."

Janet laughed. "The Personnel Department works in strange and mysterious ways. I've learned that it's easier not to question their motives. Just fill out the forms and smile." The dark-haired woman laughed as if Janet had just told an extremely funny joke.

"Now, Jo," Janet continued. "You'll have to get acquainted with the way we do things around here. So, I've asked Dacey"—Janet pointed to the dark-haired woman—"to fill you in on all the procedures. Dacey's my Assistant Editor and she knows all the ropes."

"I thought, if you're free, we could have lunch together today." Dacey smiled sweetly at Jo as she lit another cigarette.

"That would be great," Jo replied.

"Fine," said Janet. "And, Jo, just for your information, I have a strict rule about your working hours. If I work late, I expect you to do likewise. Neither of you"—Janet pointed first to Jo then to Dacey—"leaves the office until I do. Dacey knows that already, but I wanted you, Jo, to be perfectly clear about your hours so we have no misunderstandings."

Jo nodded solemnly.

"Okay, you two go talk and then take a quick lunch. Murphy and I will be working through lunch in order to -

finish his novel." Janet pointed to the huge manuscript perched on top of all the paraphernalia on her desk. "Murphy should be typing away next door. We've got a load of revisions to make on his last chapter."

Remembering her date with Roarke that night, Jo's heart seemed to skip a beat. She wondered if she should tell Janet about it but decided not to. This didn't seem like the time or the place to bring up a personal matter.

Janet started turning the pages of Roarke's manuscript, signaling that the meeting was over. Both Dacey and Jo rose at the same time and left the office together.

At Jo's desk, Dacey spent several minutes explaining the phone system, telling her how to make local and long-distance calls, identifying which extensions went into which offices and such. Jo took mental notes and hoped the phones wouldn't get really active until she had the system down pat. Then Dacey quickly reviewed for Jo several other basic office procedures.

About an hour later, Dacey suggested that they leave for lunch. She took Jo to a small Japanese restaurant two blocks away from the office. Jo had never eaten Japanese food, but she didn't mind experimenting. After all, exotic lunches were going to become a normal occurrence in her new life. In the restaurant, Dacey and Jo were seated at a tiny table near the front window.

"This is the best sushi restaurant in New York," Dacey said emphatically as she wiggled out of her bulky coat.

"Great," Jo replied, wondering what "sushi" meant but too embarrassed to ask.

The menu offered little help to Jo since it was written mainly in Japanese. Jo was reluctant to question the menu, figuring she'd seem like a country bumpkin compared to the sophisticated Dacey. "Since you know the restaurant so well," Jo said, "why don't you order lunch for both of us?"

"Okay." Dacey quickly gave the Oriental waitress their order.

The two women made small talk until the waitress approached the table with their lunch. She placed a small wooden board in front of Jo.

"Here's your sushi." The waitress pointed to several small rolls of rice wrapped in seaweed and a few slivers of raw fish artfully arranged on the board. Dacey began eating her identical platter, deftly wielding her chopsticks. Shyly, Jo asked the waitress for a fork.

An uneasy silence settled between the two women as they ate their lunch. The sushi had a delicate salty taste that Jo rather liked. Dacey and Jo sipped weak green tea.

"How many books a year does Janet publish?" Jo asked in order to break the silence.

"Oh, Janet and I publish about a dozen a year, I guess," Dacey replied as she lit a cigarette. "Of course, Murphy Roarke accounts for most of our profits. He's Janet's biggest author so she spends a lot of time with him." Dacey laughed. "Not that he *needs* that much editing, if you get my drift."

Jo stared blankly at Dacey. "I don't know what you mean," she said innocently.

"Well, you will. Just wait till you meet Mr. Roarke." Dacey flicked her ashes into the plastic ashtray.

"I was introduced to him yesterday," Jo said as nonchalantly as possible. "He seemed quite friendly."

Dacey laughed again, smoke streaming from her nostrils. "I'll say he's friendly. In fact, he and Janet are extremely friendly."

"Well, they must have to work very closely together. What's wrong with their being good friends?" Slowly Jo realized what Dacey was implying. "But I thought," Jo blurted out and then paused. "Isn't Janet married?" Jo asked casually. She played with the paper wrapper from the chopsticks. "I mean, aren't those photographs of her children in her office?"

Dacey shook her head in disbelief. "I can see you have a lot to learn about publishing in New York." Dacey chuckled as she extinguished her cigarette.

Jo felt dizzy. Was Murphy Roarke having an affair with Janet Tarlin? If so, how would Janet react if she knew Roarke had made a date with Jo? Hoping Dacey's remarks were just idle gossip, Jo pushed these thoughts out of her mind. She wanted to change the subject as quickly as possible.

Jo refilled their teacups. "Do you edit any books yourself?" she asked Dacey.

"Of course I do. When Janet is busy I do a lot of editing. Right now I'm working on a fabulous cookbook. Oriental cooking. That's why I'm into Japanese food these days."

The waitress returned to their table, removed the wooden platters and deposited the check on the table. Jo blanched when she saw the bill. She had just enough money to cover her share.

"I guess we'd better be getting back to the office," Dacey said with a yawn. She reached over the table and grabbed the check. The amount on the bill didn't seem to faze her at all. Jo handed her half to Dacey, who paid the waitress.

On the short walk back to the office, Jo realized that she'd given *all* her money to Dacey. She could go to the bank near her hotel early tomorrow morning, but that meant she'd have to walk home from work (almost forty blocks) after her drink with Murphy tonight. She couldn't possibly borrow money from him on their first date. Somehow, Jo would have to get used to New York prices. Ten dollars for lunch! In Falls Creek Jo could lunch for a week on ten dollars.

Trying not to think about her precarious financial position, Jo sat down at her desk and started sorting through the stack of afternoon mail. After opening all the envelopes and piling the letters in order of importance, she turned to her electric typewriter and began typing the letters Janet had dictated sometime earlier. Jo was fully absorbed in her typing when she felt a hand tapping her on the shoulder.

"Joanna, I've been calling you for five minutes," Janet Tarlin said, standing over Jo's chair.

"Oh, I'm sorry, Mrs. Tarlin," Jo quickly removed her headset. "I didn't hear you with these earplugs on."

"Yes, so I see. Well, I want you in my office; I've something for you to do." Janet turned briskly and Jo followed her into the corner office.

With his back towards the office door, Murphy Roarke stood staring out of Janet's window. His left hand rubbed the back of his neck. He stretched out both arms and arched his back, causing his pale blue sweater to rise up several inches. His faded jeans hugged the muscular contour of his thighs.

Still stretching, he turned slowly and smiled at Jo. "Hello again, Joanna," he said.

"Hello, Mr. Roarke," Jo said formally. Dacey's gossip at lunch had left her more uncertain than ever about how to act in his presence.

He cocked an eyebrow at the tone of her voice. "How's it going on your first day at Harris House?" he asked, tugging on the border of his sweater.

"Very well, thank you. I'm a bit confused, but I'm happy to be here." Jo had to force herself not to stare at his muscular body.

"Good. But remember: be careful of all the bright young sharks out there." Murphy gestured with his head towards the desks outside of Janet's office. Confused, Joanna turned her head and peeked outside. All she saw was Dacey, standing beside Jo's desk and looking through the stack of mail Jo had just opened and sorted.

"What do you mean?" Jo asked innocently. After all, Dacey was probably only checking on the job of mail-sorting Jo had recently completed.

"Oh, Murph, for heaven's sake!" Janet exclaimed. "Will you stop that nonsense? It's only Joanna's first day and I don't want you making her nervous." Janet shook her head in disapproval as she sat down behind her desk. "I think I'd like it better if you two hadn't met yet," she mumbled.

Murphy shrugged his shoulders and sat down on Janet's small couch.

Totally confused, Jo sat down slowly on the chair opposite Janet's desk. What in the world did Roarke mean by "the bright young sharks out there"? She felt a wave of insecurity wash over her.

Jo crossed her legs. Unconsciously, she was swinging her left leg out over her right leg. She stole a glance at Roarke and noticed him staring at her ankles. Immediately, she stopped the nervous kicking movement.

Meanwhile, Janet was leafing through Murphy's manuscript. "The good news this afternoon is that Murphy and I have finally finished the corrections on *The Finlandia Affair*." Janet began placing the manuscript pages in a big box. "But we've messed up the page numbers so I'll need you to repaginate the manuscript for me, Joanna." Janet handed the box of manuscript pages to Jo and grabbed her coat off the coatrack behind her desk. "Murphy and I are celebrating by having a drink at '21,' so take care of the phones and I'll see you tomorrow." Janet pointed to Murphy's novel. "Just have that paginated by tomorrow morning." Janet turned to Murphy, who hadn't moved off the couch. She smiled flirtatiously at him. "I'll meet you by the elevators, Murph," she said. "I have one quick stop to make before we leave." Janet turned and hurried out of the office.

Murphy got up slowly from the couch and crossed the room to Jo's side. "I think there's about six hundred pages, but I can't be sure after all the cutting Janet did. Naturally, she's deleted my favorite scene between the hero and his grandfather." He sighed. "Ah, what we artists have to suffer at the hands of our editors," he said jokingly.

Murphy hadn't mentioned their drink date that night and Jo suspected he'd forgotten all about it. She was too shy to bring it up. "I'd better get to work on this right away." She started to move toward the door. "I feel a little bit overwhelmed."

"Don't worry, you'll be fine in this job. Just take it one day at a time."

"And what about those 'sharks' you mentioned?"

He laughed. "Well, whenever you're treading in deep waters, it's wise to watch out for whoever's swimming behind you."

Their eyes locked together for a moment. For the first

time, Jo noticed that Roarke's eyes were like pure black discs; the pupils were barely distinguishable in color from his irises. She had never seen such compelling eyes before.

"You'd better hurry," she said nervously. "Janet must be waiting for you by now."

"You're probably right," he sighed. Roarke grabbed his pea coat off the rack and flung it over his arm. He started for the door before turning suddenly to Jo.

"Wait a minute," he said slowly. "In all the excitement of finishing *Finlandia,* I forgot all about our date."

"Oh, that's okay," Jo said quickly. She lifted the manuscript box for a moment. "This pagination job will take me a while to finish anyway."

"No, it's not all right. And I'm getting pretty disgusted with myself for apologizing to you all the time. Listen, are you free tomorrow night for dinner? I'll cook. My place."

Jo blinked. Murphy Roarke was going to cook dinner for her? "You don't have to go to all that trouble for me," she said.

"I know I don't. I want to. And I promise you, I'm a very good cook," he said. "Really, it'll be fun."

"Well, if you're sure it's not too much trouble."

"I'm positive." He dropped his coat on the chair and scrawled his address on a piece of scrap paper from Janet's desk. "My apartment is in the Village and it's not hard to find. Here's the address." He handed her the piece of paper. "I'll see you tomorrow night around seven."

"Is there anything I can bring?"

"Yes, you can bring your good appetite and your good looks," he joked as he walked over to Jo.

Jo was still holding his manuscript, so she couldn't

reach out to him. Before she knew what was happening, he leaned over and kissed her on the lips. His mouth was warm and moist, with a faintly salty taste. The kiss seemed to linger for a long time but it left Jo yearning for it to last even longer.

"Happy Birthday, Joanna E. Davenport," he whispered in her ear. Before she could respond he picked up his coat and walked through the door. Jo was left standing with his manuscript, her mouth hanging open in astonishment.

She walked slowly back to her desk, laying the heavy box on her chair. She touched her finger lightly to her mouth where she could still feel his lips on hers. The warm tingling feeling was delightful, and she wished she could indulge herself in thinking about it. But she was worried about her attraction for Roarke. Although she didn't quite believe Dacey's gossip, she couldn't help worrying about what would happen if there were some truth to the rumor.

3

With a flip of her hand, Joanna waved hello to Lila, the receptionist at Harris House, as she hurried into the offices the next morning. Jo was a half-hour late for work. Everything had gone wrong. Her navy skirt had needed mending, the lines at her bank were endlessly long, and the subway downtown had stalled mid-tunnel.

With a loud *thump* Jo dropped Roarke's manuscript and her purse on her desk. She flung off her coat, draped it over the back of her chair and peeked into Janet's office. Unfortunately, Janet had already arrived at work. She was sitting behind her cluttered desk, reading *The New York Times* and sipping coffee from a paper cup.

Jo picked up Roarke's manuscript and hurried into Janet's office. "Good morning, Mrs. Tarlin," she said cheerfully.

"Good morning, dear," Janet Tarlin responded. Her

eyes darted towards Jo and then returned quickly to the paper.

"I'm sorry I'm late getting to work this morning," Jo said shyly. "I had to go to the bank and then my subway broke down and, well, it's just been one of those mornings."

Janet put down the newspaper. "That's okay, Jo. Here, sit down and calm yourself. I ride the subway myself so I know how it goes. You can't let it upset you.

"Anyway, I'm in a good mood this morning after reading Rakovich's column." Janet pointed to the *Times*. "Have you seen it yet?"

"No," Jo answered, a little embarrassed because she'd never heard of Rakovich.

"Oh, you must, it's a marvelous piece. Today's topic is the Israeli bombing in Iraq." Janet shook her head. "I'm convinced that Misha Rakovich is the sole honest columnist in print, even though I don't always agree with his point of view."

"How's that?" Jo asked politely.

"Well, you can't label him. He's neither right wing, liberal, moderate nor conservative. Every column he writes deals strictly with the issue at hand. He evaluates each issue individually." Janet pointed a finger at Jo. "That's a very rare quality for a journalist." Janet sighed as she tossed the newspaper into her open briefcase. "I'd give almost anything to publish a book by Rakovich. I wouldn't care what topic he wanted to cover, if only I could get him to write a book for Harris House. Aside from the fact that any book by Misha would be an important one, he has such a devoted following, I'm sure he'd sell like hotcakes in hardcover."

"Have you approached him with an offer?" Jo asked.

Janet laughed. "Well, it's rather difficult to approach a phantom." Janet squinted at Jo. "You do know about Rakovich's reputation, don't you?"

Jo shook her head. Janet seemed amazed. "Well, no one's ever met Rakovich, as far as I know," Janet began. "His columns first appeared in the *Times* about three years ago. Misha seemed to have appeared from out of thin air.

"Rumor has it that Misha escaped from behind the Iron Curtain, but that's just speculation. The publicity department at the *Times* claims that he has to keep his identity a secret because his work is very controversial and his sources for information are extremely sensitive. CIA and KGB, I suspect.

"Anyway, no one's been able to track him down although everyone in publishing has tried. There's not a house in New York that wouldn't jump at the chance to publish a book by Rakovich."

Jo was intrigued. "This may sound naive, but doesn't he have an office at the *Times?* Someone there must see him coming and going."

"Yes, he has an office, but nobody's ever seen him behind his desk. There's a very nice secretary who handles his calls and mail."

"Have you tried talking to her?"

"Talking to her?" Janet scoffed. "I've taken that redhead to lunch four times. The first thing she ever said to me was that she'd never met Rakovich in person. Her contact with him is strictly through friends of his who act as messengers.

"At first, I didn't believe her, but now I think she's telling the truth. At our last lunch, I plied her with Bloody Marys for two hours, and she still stuck to her story.

Either she's telling the truth, or she's a closet alcoholic."
Janet laughed.

"I wish I could help you contact this Rakovich," Jo said
thoughtfully.

"So do I. I'd promote you on the spot if you could get
him for my list," Janet said emphatically.

"I doubt it will do any good, but if you want to try
talking to Doris, his secretary, then go ahead. Who
knows? Maybe she'll talk to someone her own age more
easily than she'd talk to me." Janet shrugged. "Let me
know if you come up with anything."

Janet picked up her phone, cradled the receiver on her
left shoulder and started dialing. "Is that Murphy's
manuscript?" she asked, pointing to the box in Jo's hand.

"Yes," Jo replied. "I took it home last night and
finished the pagination for you. It's six hundred and
fifty-two pages long."

"Good," said Janet. "Just leave it on the chair." Janet
made a quick note on her desk calendar. "I think I'll
throw a party when that manuscript finally goes down to
Copyediting," she murmured.

Janet picked up her phone and began dialing, abruptly
ending her conversation with Jo.

Back at her desk, Jo took a blank piece of typing paper
and, in capital letters, she printed the name Misha
Rakovich. She underlined the name three times and
stared thoughtfully at it. If only I could get to Rakovich, Jo
thought wistfully.

How would an experienced editor approach this problem? she wondered. Somehow there had to be a way to
get to Rakovich. And, once contacted, how could he
possibly refuse an offer to publish a book in hardcover?

Wasn't it the ambition of every writer to be published by a prestigious company like Harris House?

Joanna picked up the phone. First she dialed information, and then she called the *New York Times* offices and asked for Mr. Rakovich. A woman cheerfully answered the phone.

"Misha Rakovich's office. May I help you?" the woman said.

"Yes," Joanna replied. "My name is Joanna Davenport and I'm calling from Harris House Publishers. I'd like to speak to Mr. Rakovich please."

The woman on the other end of the phone chuckled. "I'm afraid that's impossible. Can I ask what this call is in reference to?"

"Well, it's rather personal. Could I leave my name and number? Would you ask Mr. Rakovich to return my call, please?" Jo tried to sound as authoritative as possible.

"Sure. I'd be happy to take the information, but if you're calling to get Mr. Rakovich to write a book for Harris House, there's not much hope that he'll return your call."

"Why not?" Jo asked innocently.

"Well, he gets quite a few calls like this one and he never returns them, as far as I know. He doesn't seem interested in writing a book. I'm sorry but that's just how he is." The woman seemed genuinely sympathetic to Jo.

"I understand; there's no need for you to apologize. It's certainly not your fault. I'd appreciate it if you'd give him the message that I called." Jo repeated her name and phone number before saying goodbye.

Jo had just hung up the receiver when the phone rang. "Janet Tarlin's office," she said absentmindedly, still thinking about the mysterious Rakovich.

"Good morning," a male voice sang out. "I'd like to speak to the beautiful new lady at Harris House."

"I beg your pardon." Jo was jolted out of her thoughts by the playful voice.

"A beautiful lady. I need to speak to a beautiful lady. I hear there's a new one working for Janet Tarlin these days."

"Who is this?" Jo said angrily.

"How quickly they forget!" The man sighed, chuckling deeply. Jo instantly recognized the throaty laughter.

"Roarke!" she exclaimed. "Is that you?"

"Who else were you expecting after that introduction?"

She laughed. "You're right. I should've known it could only have been you."

"I'm calling to confirm our date tonight. I've just put a gorgeous piece of beef on the stove. You're in for a rare treat tonight. Not everyone gets to taste my Beef Stroganoff. I trust you'll be sufficiently impressed with the results."

"Oh, I'm sure it'll be wonderful but . . . about tonight. I'm afraid that I can't make it." Jo tried to sound convincing.

"That's too bad. Are you sure?"

"Yes, you see, something important came up, and I have to work late tonight." Jo could feel her cheeks burning. She was grateful that this conversation was taking place over the phone, she couldn't have fabricated this excuse if she had to face him.

Roarke sighed. "Well, I suppose you'll just miss out on my little surprise," he said.

"What's that?" Jo asked, her curiosity instantly aroused.

"I was going to save this for tonight, but I happen to know of an inexpensive apartment that may be available for subleasing."

"Where?"

Roarke chuckled. "Oh no. You'll have to come to dinner to find that out."

"But that's blackmail!"

"Damned right," he exclaimed. "These circumstances call for radical measures."

In spite of herself, Jo couldn't help giggling. He sounded so appealing over the phone, her resolve to stay away from him slowly disintegrated.

"You're not going to get out of this dinner," he said firmly. "I simply won't hear of it. You'll be here at seven o'clock, or I'll cancel my latest contract with Harris House."

"Oh, Murphy, be serious. It's just . . . well, I've been thinking that . . ."

"Don't think. It gets you into all kinds of trouble. Just do." He lowered his voice to a whisper. "Trust your instincts, Joanna. In matters like this, there's no better guide."

Jo licked her dry lips. "Okay," she said weakly. "I'll be there at seven."

"Terrific!" he exclaimed. "And don't worry so much. We'll have a wonderful dinner, and I'll be a perfect gentleman. Unless requested to be otherwise." He laughed as he hung up the phone.

Jo didn't have time to think about his last comment. Immediately after his call, Janet asked Jo and Dacey into her office. For the next several hours, Janet reviewed the manuscript submissions that had accumulated during the week.

Most of the submissions were returned, unread, to their hopeful authors. Jo couldn't help feeling sorry for the authors of these novels. The only writers who even had a chance of being considered for publication were the ones lucky enough to have friends or relatives of Janet Tarlin. Janet paid attention to the manuscripts that mentioned a familiar name in their covering letters.

After the editorial meeting, Jo typed Janet's correspondence and as she worked steadily, the hours slipped by. She was startled when she caught sight of Janet packing up her briefcase and pulling on her leather gloves. Janet waved at Jo as she hurried out of the office. Dacey left a few minutes later. Glancing at her watch, Jo discovered it was after six o'clock. She gasped. Her date with Roarke was in less than an hour.

Jo hurried to the ladies' room with her purse in hand. She splashed cold water on her face. Quickly, she secured the heavy golden braids wound around her head. Her hand was trembling as she applied a touch of pale lipstick and dabbed a little rouge on her cheeks, the only make-up she ever wore. She didn't know if she was trembling because she hadn't slept last night or because she was on her way to Murphy Roarke's apartment.

It was the height of the rush hour as Jo rode a packed subway to West Fourth Street. After asking a police officer for directions, she found Roarke's building among the crisscrossed streets in the Village. Roarke lived in a narrow brownstone on Carmine Street. Like many of the surrounding buildings, the brownstone had originally been constructed as a one-family residence but had since been broken up into several apartments.

A small brass plaque was attached to the red brick facade of Roarke's building. It read: "Built in 1843, this building was the one-time residence of John Philip Sousa. This address has been declared a landmark building by the City of New York."

Jo rang Roarke's bell and peeked through the small glass window in the middle of the ornate door. She could see Roarke walking down the darkly carpeted hallway. He wore a clean white apron over faded jeans and a red T-shirt.

Jo wished she'd had time to run back to her hotel room and change out of her work clothes. She was still wearing her navy skirt, white sweater, and stockings. The outfit was fine for the office but, after seeing Roarke through the window, she felt as if she were dressed too formally. However, it was too late to think about her outfit now.

Roarke was wiping his hands on the front of his apron as he pulled open the door. He smiled when he saw Jo standing on the steps.

"I'm so glad you decided to come." He smiled as he took her elbow and led her down the hall to his apartment.

"You didn't tell me you lived in a landmark building," Jo said.

"You mean the plaque outside?" He chuckled. "Yes, on rainy nights the ghost of John Philip Sousa blasts his tuba down these hallowed hallways."

Jo giggled. Roarke still had his hand on her arm as Jo

fumbled with the buttons on her coat. "Well, I hope I'm not too early. I mean, too late. The subway seemed to take forever." She wondered if she looked as nervous as she felt.

He shook his head. "Nope, you're right on time. And you look smashing tonight." He took her shoulder and gently forced her to turn around as he inspected her from head to toe. "You should always wear white next to your face, it becomes you," he said in a whisper.

As always when she received a compliment, Jo's cheeks blushed with color. The rosy flush added a glow to her velvet skin and Roarke stood mesmerized, staring at her. His obvious admiration embarrassed her. Jo didn't consider herself especially attractive. She took her looks for granted, and it was always a surprise when she attracted attention from men.

"Where should I put my coat?" She turned to avoid his dark eyes.

"Throw it anywhere," he said. "I've got to check on the Stroganoff." He released her arm and hurried into the kitchen.

Jo placed her coat on a wingback chair as she inspected Roarke's home. Apparently, his apartment took up the entire first floor of the brownstone.

The large living room had a sixteen-foot ceiling with elaborately carved moldings. Two huge French windows looked out over the street and a fire was blazing in the marble fireplace.

Murphy's furniture was an eclectic mixture of antique Victorian and Art Deco, combining golden oak and gleaming chrome. Each piece was unique, but it all blended together elegantly. Bookshelves climbed from floor to ceiling, covering almost every wall. The apartment was a virtual library.

"What can I get you to drink?" Murphy called out from the kitchen. "How about a little white wine?"

"That would be fine," Jo said as she walked into the kitchen.

The tiny kitchen was little more than a closet-sized passageway between the living room and the bedroom in the rear of the apartment. But the small space didn't seem to inhibit Roarke's movements. He looked perfectly at home in the minuscule space, moving gracefully from the bubbling pots on the stove to the opened bottle of wine on top of the refrigerator. He handed a wineglass to Jo.

"Cheers!" he said, clinking glasses with Jo. "And welcome to my humble abode."

"Hardly humble at all," Jo responded as she sipped her wine. "You have a fabulous apartment. May I see the rest of it?"

His dark eyes twinkled. "Why, certainly. I'd be delighted to show you my bedroom. I was hoping you'd ask."

He took her hand and led her into the bedroom. Even though she knew he was kidding, she could feel the muscles behind her knees trembling. She fumbled for something, anything, to say which would disguise her agitation.

"This apartment is sensational," she said. "I wish I were lucky enough to find a place like this."

The walls of Roarke's bedroom, like those in the living room, were decorated in floor-to-ceiling bookshelves. Between the two bedroom windows an ornate brass bed was neatly covered with a colorful patchwork quilt. A carved oak dresser and navy Persian rug added a cozy warmth to the room. Jo complimented Roarke on his furniture and then they returned to the kitchen.

"So, where's this apartment you mentioned on the phone?" Jo asked as she followed Roarke into the kitchen.

"Upstairs." Roarke pointed to the ceiling. "My neighbor just moved to Colorado for a year. He wanted to sublet his apartment but he couldn't find a tenant. I've been watching the place for him. I'm sure it'll be okay if you live there for a few months." Roarke dipped a ladle into a large pot and skimmed off a layer of fat.

"You mean the apartment's in this building?" Jo stammered.

"Upstairs usually means within the same building," he replied with a laugh. "Why? Does that bother you?" He turned to look at her.

"No, no, of course not. It's just that I'm a little surprised." Actually, Jo was more than surprised; she was astonished.

The thought of being Roarke's neighbor set her mind racing. This would confuse everything.

I'll just take a quick look and make up some excuse for not taking it, Jo thought to herself. I'm not going to get involved with this man. I'm going to stay as far away from him as possible.

"So, when can I see this apartment?" Jo asked, anxious to get this ordeal over with.

"Whenever it's convenient for you. But I'm sure you'll want it." He shrugged.

Jo marveled at his constant self-confidence. "Then maybe I should see it right now."

"I had a feeling you'd say that." He turned off the flame under his pots, removed his apron and led Jo up to the second floor of the brownstone. With a key from the pocket of his jeans, Roarke unlocked the door at the rear of the hall.

They entered a studio apartment half the size of Roarke's place, actually, the exact size of his bedroom. In sharp contrast to Roarke's apartment, there wasn't a book in the room, only a neatly made iron bed, a gray-and-rose area rug, a table with two Shaker-style wood chairs, and a small Victorian sofa. "Your neighbor certainly is neat," Jo observed.

The apartment was very clean, almost austere, but peaceful in an uncluttered way. A large black marble fireplace added charm to the room. Two large windows overlooked a garden. There was a tiny kitchen, the same size as Roarke's, on one side of the studio and a bathroom with a clawfoot tub on the left.

"It's really a nice apartment," Jo said begrudgingly. Unfortunately it would have been a perfect apartment for her. "But I'm sure I can't afford it," she sighed.

"How much can you afford?" Murphy asked.

"I was hoping to find a place for around two hundred a month," Jo said uncertainly. The rent on this apartment was probably three times that.

"Well, you're in luck. This studio rents for one-eighty." Roarke handed her a key. "It's yours."

"Just like that?" Jo stared at the key in her hand.

"Just like that," he enthused.

"But I don't know if I should take it."

"Why not?" he asked.

Jo was much too embarrassed to reveal her feelings

about living so close to him. She couldn't really think of a reason why she should pass up this extraordinary opportunity. "I don't know," she said with a shrug of her shoulders. "I guess you're right. Why not? It's a great apartment and I'll take it. This was really nice of you. I don't know how to thank you," she added.

"I'll think of a way. After the Stroganoff. Come on."

They walked back to his apartment. Jo wanted to leap around Roarke's living room, she was so elated about her new apartment. She kept turning the key over in the palm of her hand as if she couldn't believe it was real.

"You know, I rather like the idea of having you on top of me every night," he said, pointing to the ceiling.

She blushed deeply and he chuckled.

"You really do blush easily," he said suddenly. Naturally, the remark made Jo's cheeks even redder.

"Hey! Don't be embarrassed. The problem with most women in New York is that nothing makes them blush anymore." Roarke shook his head. "New York has a way of squeezing the lifeblood out of people." He shook his head in disgust as he turned and walked into the kitchen.

Jo noticed the taut muscles of his thighs as he bent over the small icebox.

"Go sit down on the couch with your wine," he said. "I'll get our dinner on the table. I don't know about you, but I'm starving."

Instead of sitting down on the couch, Jo scanned the shelves of books in the living room while Roarke worked in the kitchen. Most of his books were non-fiction—political and historical works. Jo assumed Roarke used the books as background for his novels.

She couldn't help noticing the books piled on his oak

rolltop desk. Obviously, these were the works he'd been reading most recently. Of the dozen or so volumes on the desk, half concerned the history of Israel and the other half were about the politics of Iraq. They reminded Jo of the article in the *Times* by Misha Rakovich.

"I see you're reading about the politics of the Middle East," she commented as they sat down at the dinner table.

He nodded, piling her plate with noodles.

"I guess that's for your next novel?"

"Well," he hesitated. "I really don't like to talk about my current projects. It's bad luck." He shrugged. "You know, you're beginning to sound a lot like an editor."

Taking the remark as a compliment, she smiled. "I didn't mean to pry; the books on your desk reminded me of a problem that came up at work today." Jo tasted the stew. "Um, this is a delicious Stroganoff."

"Thanks, it's an old family recipe. The secret's in the sour cream." He sipped his wine. "What's your problem at the office?"

"I'm sure you're familiar with Misha Rakovich, the columnist from the *Times*."

Murphy's eyebrows shot up at the mention of the Russian name. "Yes, I read Rakovich every now and then."

Jo helped herself to a large serving of Roarke's endive salad. "Well, Mrs. Tarlin reads him religiously. She's really anxious to publish a book by him. She's tried every which way to contact him, but he's unreachable. They call him the 'Phantom of the Newsroom,' you know."

"The guy's entitled to his privacy, if that's what he wants."

Jo was startled by the gruff tone of his voice.

"Sorry," he said. "I didn't mean it to sound that way." He poured himself another glass of wine. "What kind of book does Janet want Rakovich to write?"

"I don't think she cares what he writes," Jo shrugged. "She just wants him on our list." They both grinned when Jo said "our list." It sounded only natural for her to include herself in the publishing program at Harris House. "Anyway," she continued, "I would really like to get Rakovich for Janet. She practically guaranteed me a promotion if I can do it." Jo pointed her fork for emphasis.

"Then go after him," Roarke said simply.

"But how? I can't even speak to him on the phone. No one gets past his secretary."

Mimicking the "Godfather" voice of Marlon Brando, Roarke growled, "Make him an offer he can't refuse."

"Oh, that's great advice." Jo giggled. "I suppose you have another neighbor who'll break Misha's legs for the glory of Harris House."

Roarke burst out laughing. "No, sorry. Don't know anyone like that. Besides, that's not the kind of offer I had in mind. What I meant was that you should offer him something too good to pass up."

"Money?" Jo asked uncertainly.

"No. Although money's usually a good incentive, I'm sure Misha's already been offered big advance money. Look, if you're going to work with writers, you have to start thinking like one. Now, what do authors hate more than anything else?" Roarke asked.

Jo twirled her wineglass by its stem before answering him. It was difficult to concentrate with Roarke's coal black eyes boring into her, but she knew he was trying to help her.

"Editors?" she said with a short laugh.

He shook his head. "I quote P.G. Wodehouse: 'Authors as a class are not men who like to work,'" he said seriously.

"In other words, writers hate to write," Jo said thoughtfully.

"Exactly!" Roarke nodded. "Offer Rakovich a chance to publish a book in hardcover without having to do any more work. Now, there's an offer no self-respecting writer could refuse."

"But how?" Jo thought for a moment. "Um, I suppose we could publish a collection of his columns in an anthology. Then he wouldn't have to do any additional writing."

"Good thinking," Roarke said. He spooned another helping of the stew onto his plate. "Who knows?" He shrugged. "It just might be the right offer."

"Yes," she murmured hopefully. "Wouldn't that be something? I'll write him a letter tomorrow morning and suggest it. Janet will be so pleased to hear your idea," she added.

At the mention of Janet's name, Roarke abruptly paused, his fork held midair. He glanced quickly at Joanna and then slowly placed his fork on the edge of his plate.

"You know, Joanna, it might be better if you left out my name when you talk to Janet."

Jo's suspicions were instantly aroused. What was Roarke trying to hide?

Joanna nibbled on a piece of French bread. "Why

shouldn't I include you when I tell Janet the idea about Misha?" she asked demurely. "Without you, it would never have occurred to me."

"You might as well take credit for it yourself." He shrugged. "It'll help your career more than mine."

Jo laughed. "Well, I can't argue with that." She spent a few seconds trying to frame her next question so it wouldn't sound like she was prying into his personal life. "Maybe you could give me another piece of advice," she began.

"Sure, I'd be happy to help, if I can," he replied as he refilled her wine glass.

"Well, I've been wondering about Janet. What's she really like?" Jo pushed her plate towards the center of the table; she was more interested in Murphy's answer than in eating any more supper.

Roarke glanced at Jo suspiciously. "Janet's probably the best editor in New York, if that's what you mean. She's a tough lady to work for," Roarke shook his head, "but I wouldn't want anyone else editing my books."

"I know she's a good editor, but I was wondering about her personal life. She's happily married, isn't she?"

"Yes, as far as I know." Roarke avoided Jo's green eyes. "What makes you ask?"

"Oh, I don't know. Just the usual office gossip that gets passed around." Jo was hoping Roarke would question the nature of the office gossip and then, perhaps, she could discern the validity of the rumor from his answer. If there's an ounce of truth in Dacey's gossip about Janet and Roarke, then I'd better know it now, Jo thought to herself.

"Really, Joanna, you can't take office gossip seriously," Roarke said as he collected the salad bowls, scraped and stacked the plates. "Who knows where these rumors start?" Holding the dinner plates, Roarke started towards the kitchen. "I'm surprised you pay attention to that kind of talk, Joanna. Janet's personal life is no one's business, including yours."

His brow curled thoughtfully. Walking back to Jo, he took her hand and held it between both of his. "Look, there's no great significance to my suggestion that you shouldn't mention my name to Janet or Dacey. Especially Dacey." His voice was gentle and his words came out slowly, as if he were explaining something patiently to a child.

"I make it a habit to avoid any cause for office gossip," he continued. "All you have to do is casually mention someone's name at Harris House and everyone assumes you're sleeping with him. My advice is based solely on my gut instinct. If you want to disregard it, then forget I said anything." He continued to hold her hand as if waiting for her response.

She could feel the hard calluses on his hands. It was difficult to concentrate with Roarke standing so close. She gently pulled her hand out of his, picked up the stacked salad bowls, and carried them into the kitchen.

She wondered whether he had protested too much. He hadn't really answered her question about his relationship with Janet, he'd merely avoided the issue. However, Jo obviously couldn't pursue the topic any longer.

Reminding herself again how important her job was to her—and her mother—Jo resolved not to get involved any further with Roarke until she knew for certain that it wouldn't jeopardize her position with Janet.

She sighed deeply, regretting the decision almost

immediately. "Okay, if you say so, I won't mention your name to Janet or Dacey. I'll trust your instincts, for the moment at least. Anyway, thanks for the advice."

He seemed relieved as he strode into the kitchen. "You're welcome," he said, tossing the silverware into the sink and turning to her. The kitchen was so tiny they were practically touching. Murphy leaned over and kissed her lightly on the lips. The unexpected embrace sent a shiver up her spine.

"Can I help with the dishes?" she asked, grabbing a dishtowel to disguise her nervousness.

"No," he replied. "It's easier to clean up myself. Go pour some brandy for us in the living room. I'll have this mess cleared away in no time." Murphy stroked her cheek tenderly.

Jo gingerly sidestepped Roarke and walked into the living room. A crystal decanter of brandy and two large snifters sat on the fireplace mantel. She poured the dark, amber liquid into the goblets and placed them on the coffee table.

"I really have to be going soon," she called out to him. "It's getting late and I have to be at work tomorrow by nine."

"Can't hear you with the water running," he yelled back. "Be with you in a minute."

Jo sighed as she leaned back into the cushions on the couch. She knew she shouldn't be drinking any more liquor; her head was already spinning from the wine she'd consumed at dinner. But Roarke was taking such a long time in the kitchen, and she couldn't possibly leave until he was finished. Besides, the brandy sent a delicious warmth coursing through her veins, in much the same way as Murphy's kiss.

Jo could hear Roarke humming over the sound of rushing water. The fire crackled, casting an orange glow like the final rays of sunset.

As if she were gently sinking into an hypnotic trance, Jo slowly closed her eyes. Aside from her concerns about Roarke's relationship with Janet, which she decided to forget for the moment, Joanna Davenport was happier than she ever remembered being.

Everything about this evening with Murphy Roarke had been perfect. The companionship, the good food, the wine, the warmth of the fire, the soft cushions and Murphy's humming all blended together harmoniously. In spite of her doubts, Jo felt as if she belonged here, in this cozy room with its crackling fire. A wave of drowsiness overtook her and she yawned.

Jo couldn't fight the fatigue any longer. She lazily closed her eyes and sank deeper into the couch. Her last conscious thought was that she didn't have to worry anymore about finding an apartment.

4

Jo didn't know whether or not she was dreaming. Drifting in that twilight space between sleep and consciousness, she could hear a man humming loudly from somewhere in another room. The rich baritone voice sounded just like her father's. Jo had a vision of her father standing over a hot stove, cooking his traditional Sunday morning breakfast for the family.

Jo could actually smell the dark coffee and crisp bacon her father would lovingly prepare for her and her mother. She cuddled against the quilt, filled with the peaceful security of her childhood.

Then she remembered. Her father was gone. This must be one of the many dreams she'd experienced since he had died. Her smooth forehead wrinkled in disappointment.

She decided to get out of bed. Yawning loudly, she stretched her lithe body on the bed. Her hand unexpectedly hit a cold piece of metal. She turned her head in surprise. A ray of morning sunlight flashed off the solid brass headboard towering above her.

Joanna bolted upright, twisting her head from side to side. All she saw were bookshelves. With a start, she realized that she was sitting in Murphy Roarke's bed.

She hadn't been dreaming about the humming or the smell of coffee and bacon. Roarke was cooking breakfast in his tiny kitchen, humming in a rich baritone that sounded so much like her father's voice.

Frantically, Joanna tried to recall the events of last night. The last thing she remembered was sipping brandy on the couch in the living room. Roarke had been humming in the kitchen just as he was humming now.

What had happened since she'd drifted off to sleep last night? Afraid of what she might be wearing (or not wearing), Jo quickly glanced under the patchwork quilt covering her. She was semi-clad in her full slip and panties. Although relieved, she had to admit that the delicate lace bodice barely covered her full breasts. Her lips pursed in thoughtful deliberation.

Where had Roarke slept? she wondered frantically. Both the pillowcase and the sheet on the left side of the bed were smooth and unrumpled. Apparently, she'd slept alone in this large comfortable bed. She allowed herself one moment of relief as she fell back into her pillow.

The relief passed quickly, followed by panic. How was she going to face Roarke this morning? She pushed the thought out of her mind and forced herself out of bed.

Although she was alone in the bedroom and the door to the kitchen was tightly closed, Jo carefully draped the quilt around her body and fled into the bathroom. After a quick shower, she rubbed a dab of toothpaste across her teeth.

Her hair was still tightly braided on top of her head. She fumbled with her tortoiseshell hairpins, smoothing the unruly strands of light hair. Her cheeks were unusually flushed as if she'd applied too much rouge. She chewed her lower lip, wondering where Roarke had hidden her clothes.

Slowly, she opened the door and peered into the empty bedroom. She noticed her sweater neatly folded on the bureau, her skirt hung over the back of the oak rocking chair. Clutching the quilt around her body again, she raced to the bureau and grabbed her sweater. As she quickly slipped into the turtleneck, she pictured Roarke's hands removing her sweater while she slept soundly. Embarrassment washed over her, followed immediately by an unexpected rush of excitement. The burst of emotions forced her into action as if she'd received a jolt of electricity.

After securely fastening the waistband of her skirt, Jo walked to the bedroom door. Taking a deep breath, she opened the door and entered Roarke's kitchen.

Murphy was standing at the stove holding a spatula in one hand and a book in the other. The bacon sizzled in the frying pan while Roarke read. His coal black eyes peered over the top of the thick gray volume as Jo entered the kitchen. He raised his eyebrows playfully and smiled at her.

She stood in the doorway, afraid to move and too embarrassed to speak. Her heart was pounding wildly.

Roarke continued to stare at her with a smile on his lips. He was obviously enjoying the moment. He had stopped humming and, as if he couldn't help it, his smile stretched wider and wider over his white teeth.

Jo took another deep breath and forced her mouth to curl into a smile. "Good morning," she said as calmly as possible.

Roarke nodded. "Good morning," he replied. "Sleep well last night?" He closed the book with one hand and laid it on top of the refrigerator.

"Very well, thank you. And you?" She couldn't keep the awkward tone of formality from her voice.

"Not too bad. Although that iron bed upstairs is a bit uncomfortable." Roarke shrugged. "Soft mattress," he added.

Jo felt the muscles in her face relax into a genuine smile. The tension that had knotted her stomach since she'd awakened in Roarke's brass bed was slowly evaporating. Maybe last night wasn't such a disaster after all, she thought hopefully.

Jo decided to bluff her way through the morning.

"The bacon smells great," she said enthusiastically. "Can I help with anything?"

"Sure. Pour the coffee and I'll have food on the table in no time." Roarke turned towards the frying pan and started scooping out the crisp bacon. He placed each strip on a neatly folded paper towel.

Jo poured two mugs of steaming coffee and carried them into the living room. The table was already set with placemats and china. A small crystal vase held a bunch of yellow daisies.

He came into the living room carrying a large tray laden with a plate of bacon, a bowl of scrambled eggs, cut grapefruits, and a straw basket of toast.

"Before we eat," Roarke said as he transferred the food from the tray to the table, "let me tell you exactly what happened last night.

"By the time I finished cleaning up in the kitchen, you were fast asleep on the couch. I tried to wake you but you were out like a light. So, I carried you in there"—he pointed to the bedroom—"and put you to bed."

Joanna stared down at the eggs on her plate. They were well-done, just the way she liked them. "I'm afraid I had too much wine last night." She shrugged. "Also, I was up all night the night before, so I guess I just passed out." She took a deep breath. "Anyway, I'm sorry."

"I'm sorry, too." Roarke replied. "You missed a great dessert."

Jo looked up quickly, wondering if his remark had a double meaning. She didn't know how to respond to his comment. He was staring at her so oddly. Jo squirmed uncomfortably in her chair.

"Aren't you going to ask me how you got undressed last night?" He continued buttering his toast as if he'd inquired about the weather.

For the first time that morning, Jo met his gaze head-on. "No," she said in mock defiance, "I was going to ask you for the salt."

Roarke burst out laughing as he picked up the salt shaker. He handed it to her as if it were a trophy.

She returned his smile and breathed a sigh of relief. Roarke was taking the incident with good humor. He didn't seem at all angry about her appalling behavior last night.

"Well, I thank you for everything last night, including your wonderful Stroganoff," Jo said happily. "And I promise, next time I won't fall asleep on you."

"You'd better not," Roarke warned with a chuckle. "Next time I might not be such a gentleman."

Jo tingled at the thought but she quickly suppressed the feeling. Suddenly, she was ravenously hungry. She grabbed her fork and wolfed down her eggs.

They finished breakfast before Joanna noticed that it was already half-past eight. She'd have to hurry or she'd be late for work. Unfortunately, there wasn't time for Jo to return to her hotel room. She'd have to wear the same clothes she wore yesterday to work. Of the two evils, Jo decided being late was worse than being unfashionable.

"You'd better hurry," Roarke warned suddenly, as if he were reading her mind. "It's almost nine." He started clearing dishes off the table.

His tone was so abrupt, Jo had the fleeting suspicion he wanted her out of the apartment. She admonished herself for feeling paranoid. It *was* almost nine o'clock, and she should be leaving for work. Jo walked over to the couch and gathered up her coat and purse.

"So, when is moving day?" Roarke asked brightly, holding up Jo's coat so that she could easily slip into it.

In all the excitement this morning, she'd almost forgotten about her new apartment. "If it's okay, I'll bring my stuff around on Saturday," she said.

"Fine by me." Roarke held the front door open. "By the way"—he grinned—"last night you never gave me the chance to find out what the 'E' stands for."

"Emma," she said, shrugging. "Can you imagine? Joanna Emma? I don't know what my parents were thinking when they named me."

"Let's see. Emma, huh? Well, there's Emma Bovary, Emma Peel, and Auntie Em from the *Wizard of Oz*. You have an adulteress from *Madame Bovary*, an 'Avenger' or a farmer's wife to choose from." His eyes twinkled playfully. "Which Emma are you, Joanna?"

She glanced up at his face as he reeled off his three prototypes. Indeed, which description fit her best? More importantly, which one would he have labeled her this morning?

"I guess I'm a bit of all three," she joked.

He laughed as he bent down to kiss her. "Exactly what I would've said," he whispered huskily. His warm mouth lingered on her lips, melting away the chill morning air. He hugged her tightly. Jo's cheek felt like velvet against his face. Finally, he released her and stood staring as she walked down the street.

A light November snow was gently falling as Jo made her way to the subway station at West Fourth Street.

Jo was in high spirits by the time she arrived at Harris House. She was no longer embarrassed about falling asleep on Roarke's couch. Everything had turned out okay—Roarke wasn't angry—and the memory of awakening in Roarke's bed lingered pleasantly. That, coupled with the security of finally having her own apartment (only one flight of stairs above Roarke), made Jo feel that she was conquering New York at last.

Smiling at the strangers in the elevator, she slipped out of her coat before reaching the twentieth floor. Dacey was already typing when Jo arrived at Janet's corner of the hall.

"Good morning." Jo smiled cheerfully.

"Morning." Dacey didn't lift her head from the keyboard.

Jo hung her coat on the rack and peeked into Janet's office. It was empty. With a sigh of relief, Jo sat down at her desk and sorted the morning mail. In a few minutes, she laid a stack of neatly folded letters on Janet's desk.

Then she handed Dacey the remainder of the mail and turned her attention to the day's workload. The first thing she wanted to do was write to Misha Rakovich.

A letter to the Russian writer had been composing itself in her head since last night when she'd discussed him with Murphy. It took about an hour to handwrite a rough draft. The typed letter was ready to be mailed in a few minutes.

The single-page letter was straightforward. Jo introduced herself as Janet Tarlin's secretary, mentioned the interest of Harris House in publishing a book by Rakovich and suggested publishing a collection of his newspaper articles as essays in an anthology. Remembering Roarke's advice, Jo casually mentioned that Rakovich wouldn't have to do any additional writing to publish the collection. If he was interested in the idea, he should contact her; if not, he could disregard her inquiry.

Jo put the envelope aside, hoping to discuss the idea with Janet before mailing the letter. Since the letter made a commitment on the part of Harris House, Jo wanted to clear it with Janet before assuming the responsibility of making an offer to Rakovich.

However, Janet had not yet arrived at the office and it was almost noon. Jo asked Dacey where Janet could possibly be this late.

"Oh, I'm sorry. I forgot to tell you. Janet called very early today to say she'd be tied up with an author all morning." Dacey stroked her chin thoughtfully, staring at Jo but with a faraway expression in her eyes. "I'll bet it's Murphy Roarke," she said suddenly, winking at Jo.

Jo was startled by the mention of Roarke's name. Immediately, her guard was up. "What's Murphy Roarke?" she inquired nonchalantly.

"I'll bet Janet was meeting Roarke this morning. Janet's always setting up these morning sessions with Roarke that go on endlessly. If you ask me, Janet does it purposely so she can spend all day at his apartment." Dacey lifted her eyebrows conspiratorially. "All her other authors are called in here for office meetings," she added to prove her point.

At first Jo was relieved that Dacey hadn't associated *her* with Roarke. But the relief soon disappeared.

Jo remembered how eager Roarke had been to get her out of his apartment by nine o'clock. He must have been waiting for Janet to arrive.

Jo clenched her fists, overcome with a feeling of betrayal. Why hadn't Roarke told Jo of Janet's impending arrival? The question was too painful to consider. Jo pushed the thought out of her head and went back to typing Janet's letters.

Several hours later, Janet arrived at Harris House. Her cheeks were rosy from the cold as she brushed the snow off her full-length fur coat and matching fur hat.

"What a morning!" Janet exclaimed as she dumped her coat, hat, gloves, and briefcase on her couch. "New York is just impossible in the winter. Took me half an hour to get a cab in the Village."

Jo felt a strange tightness in her throat. So, Janet really had been at Roarke's apartment in Greenwich Village. Like a wave, jealousy washed over her. She stood staring at Janet as she riffled through the mail on her desk. Janet was seemingly unaware of the effect she was having on Jo.

"Anything important happen this morning?" Janet asked absent-mindedly.

Before Jo could reply, the phone rang and she turned to answer the call. It was one of Janet's authors. He was very upset about a recent royalty statement. Jo put him on hold and relayed the message to Janet.

"Oh, not Clayton, again," Janet moaned. "Okay, give me a few minutes to catch my breath and I'll talk to him." Janet sailed into her office.

Jo wondered if Roarke left all his women breathless as she relayed Janet's message to the man on the phone. In a few minutes, Janet picked up her extension and Jo hung up the phone.

Her hands were trembling as she returned to her typewriter. Everything had happened so quickly today. Waking up in Roarke's apartment and then discovering she'd narrowly missed bumping into her boss; it was all too much for Jo. The warm security she'd felt that morning was gone.

Wearily, she closed her eyes and rested her head on her hand. She was overcome with a longing to be back in Falls Creek, working for Ridgeway Advertising, safe from the gossip and pressure of Harris House. She almost wished she'd never met Murphy Roarke. Since he'd come into her life, everything had changed. With these thoughts in mind, it took Jo a long time to get back to Janet's dictation.

A few moments later, Dacey grabbed her coat off the hook next to her desk and walked over to Jo.

"Cover for me," she whispered. "I've got to leave early tonight."

"But what'll I tell Janet if she asks for you?" Jo stuttered.

"Oh, tell her I'm downstairs in Copyediting." Dacey flicked her hand and hurried out of the office.

Jo barely had time to take a deep breath before Janet started calling for Dacey.

Timidly, Jo approached Janet's door. "Um . . . Dacey's down in Copyediting," Jo mumbled, regretting the lie as soon as it was uttered. Lying was not a practice that came easily to Jo.

"Damn! She's always someplace else when I really need her," Janet complained loudly. "All right, Jo, come in and take this for Dacey." Janet flung a typewritten page at Jo. "When Dacey gets back from Copyediting, tell her I need her catalog copy rewritten."

Jo quickly scanned the sheet. It was a three-paragraph description of Roarke's novel, *The Finlandia Affair*.

"The marketing department just decided to make *Finlandia* a lead title," Janet announced triumphantly. "That means we'll be printing a special two-page brochure, and it's got to go to press tomorrow.

"It'll be a great push for the book. All the salesmen will get copies of the brochure for their book buyers and we'll make a big splash with it at the sales conference next week." Janet glanced at her watch and hurriedly packed her briefcase.

"I'm going to have a drink with Mr. Harris in five minutes. He wants to go over my plans for the conference." She waved her hand in disgust. "I've been presenting books at sales conferences for the past ten years, you'd think he'd trust me by now."

Janet slipped into her fur coat. "If Clayton hadn't chewed my ear off all afternoon, I'd have time to write the copy myself. Damn, where did I put my gloves?"

Jo spotted the leather gloves under Janet's couch. She retrieved them for her boss.

"Thanks," Janet said. "Tell Dacey I need that copy tomorrow morning. It's too bad if she doesn't want to work late tonight." Janet pointed her finger menacingly at Jo. "You tell her to do that rewrite or start looking for another job tomorrow. You understand, Jo?"

Jo nodded slowly.

Janet grabbed her briefcase and literally ran out of her office, scattering the loose papers on her desk as she fled.

In her hand, Jo clutched the typewritten page Janet had handed her. Immediately, Jo rushed to her phone, dialed information, and wrote down Dacey's home phone number. She dialed the number but no one answered the phone. Jo redialed. Still no answer. Every fifteen minutes, Jo dialed Dacey's apartment. By seven o'clock she wearily gave up and went home.

Using the pay phone outside her hotel room, Jo continued calling Dacey's number during the evening but she never got an answer. Finally, in desperation, Jo decided to write the copy herself. Hopefully, Jo would contact Dacey before Janet got to the office in the morning. With any luck at all, Dacey could rewrite Jo's copy before Janet discovered the deception.

Sitting down at her desk in her room, Jo thanked heaven she'd read *The Finlandia Affair* after paginating the novel the night before last. Fortunately, the novel was still fresh in her mind and Jo quickly composed a three-page description of the book.

Jo worked on the copy until midnight. Then, in her bathrobe and slippers, she crept silently to the phone in the hall. She hoped it was all right to be calling at this late hour. But she needn't have worried. No one answered Dacey's telephone.

5

Jo was at her desk by eight o'clock Friday morning. Sipping dark coffee from a paper container, she typed the expanded catalog copy from *The Finlandia Affair*. Rereading her work, Jo was pleased by how smoothly the copy read. She stapled the three pages together. Then she picked up the phone and tried dialing Dacey's number again. By now the telephone number was imprinted in her memory like a tatoo. Jo had long since given up hope of reaching Dacey but she continued calling her anyway. As expected, she got no answer at Dacey's house.

Jo checked her watch for the tenth time that morning. Nine o'clock was rapidly approaching and Janet would arrive at any moment, she thought to herself. Frantically, Jo considered discarding the *Finlandia* copy and admitting she'd lied to cover for Dacey.

On the other hand, Jo could still cover for Dacey if she

submitted the work to Janet under the pretext that Dacey had written it last night. Before Jo could decide what to do, Janet marched into the office. She strode over to Jo's desk and jabbed her finger at the typewritten pages in Jo's hand.

"That Dacey's copy?" Janet barked.

Jo froze, unable to speak.

"If it's not the copy for *Finlandia*, then where the hell is Dacey? Why isn't she at her typewriter?" Janet enunciated each word with military precision.

Jo looked down at Janet's booted foot, impatiently tapping on the linoleum. She swallowed hard, her throat excruciatingly dry. Without saying a word, Jo handed the copy to Janet.

The angry glint in Janet's eye turned first to surprise and then interest as she began reading the copy. She turned and walked into her office, never taking her eyes off Jo's copy.

Jo picked up a pencil and nervously twirled it between her fingers. She forgot about Dacey. She forgot about lying to Janet. All she thought about was whether Janet would approve her work.

Janet hadn't bothered to remove her coat as she sat down at her desk. Jo watched, fascinated, as Janet put a blue pencil to Jo's copy, slashing out lines and rewriting sentences. She resisted an impulse to rush into the corner office and protest the changes Janet was making on her copy. She forced herself to concentrate on the papers on her desk.

Jo picked up a random piece of paper. The sheet had the name "Misha Rakovich" written in her hand and underlined three times. The note, written to herself days ago, reminded Jo that she'd typed a letter to Misha yesterday. Jo started rummaging through the other papers on her desk, searching for the letter. She couldn't find it.

Jo quickly realized that Misha's letter had probably been picked up and mailed by one of the mailboys who regularly collected outgoing letters from Jo's desk. She shook her head in frustration and made a mental note to discuss the letter with Janet as soon as possible.

Now was definitely *not* the right time. Janet was hard at work on Jo's copy, totally absorbed in rewriting. She still had not removed her coat.

Suddenly, Janet looked up from her desk. She smiled and signaled Jo to come into her office.

Jo bounced off her chair and rushed to Janet's desk. Janet handed her the three pages.

"Tell Dacey I'm pleasantly surprised. Her writing is rapidly improving."

"But you've made so many changes," Jo moaned. The copy was littered with blue pencil marks.

"Minor changes in style, that's all. The copy needed a little more punch. Otherwise, it's quite well written." Janet's brow wrinkled.

"You're awfully concerned about Dacey's work," she said. "What's your stake in this?"

"Oh, nothing," Jo replied hastily. "I'm just curious about why you made these changes. I mean, I couldn't help reading the copy myself and I thought it was, well, pretty good." Jo shrugged.

"It is good. Very good. Listen, I usually have to totally rewrite every page that comes out of Dacey's typewriter." Janet pointed at the copy in Jo's hand. "Dacey will be very happy to discover how easily she's passed inspection today.

"Now, type up those corrections and get the copy down to Copyediting. Super-rush. Stand over Claire while she proofreads. Then walk the copy over to the production department." Janet dismissed Jo with a wave of her hand.

After quickly typing the copy, reluctantly adding Janet's corrections, Jo rushed it through Copyediting and delivered it to Eddie, the graphic artist who would design the brochure for Roarke's book. When she got back to Editorial, she had to run the last few yards to her desk to answer her ringing telephone.

Her heart started to pound at the sound of Roarke's voice. "Good morning, Jony Em," he said.

She blushed at the pet name he'd devised for her. "Morning, Murphy," she replied.

"You sound breathless. Did you jog to work or are you overwhelmed with excitement at hearing my voice?"

"Actually, I just ran up a flight of stairs," she said. "And the only thing that overwhelms me is your incredible ego."

He laughed. "Good, as long as you find me overwhelming, I don't care about the reason.

"Listen, I'm calling about lunch," he continued. "I'll meet you on the corner of 59th Street and Fifth Avenue at twelve thirty."

"Lunch?" she stammered. Had they made a lunch date for today? The last thing she remembered was his saying goodbye to her on the steps of his brownstone yesterday. Right before Janet arrived, a little voice whispered in her ear. Suddenly, her mood changed.

"I can't make lunch today," she said curtly. "I've got too much work."

The other extension rang. Jo started to put Roarke on

hold so she could answer the call. But then the light on the extension stopped blinking; Janet had answered the phone herself.

Murphy continued their conversation, unaware of the phone call that almost interrupted them and ignoring the sudden icy tone of Jo's voice.

"If I can give you one absolutely concrete, ironclad, irrefutable reason to meet me for lunch, will you change your mind?"

He'll never manufacture a reason that good, Jo thought to herself. "Okay. Give it your best shot," she said confidentially.

He took an exaggeratedly deep breath, pretending great anxiety. "I'll be out of town for a few days. If you want to move into the apartment upstairs, you'll have to come get the keys."

"You gave me the key when you showed me the apartment," she said triumphantly.

"I gave you the key to the apartment," he countered. "You still need the key to the front door of the building."

Jo opened her mouth to speak but before she could reply, she heard Janet screaming her name, commanding her to "Get in here this minute." Half a dozen secretaries jumped at the volume of Janet's voice.

"I gotta run," Jo said quickly. "Fifty-ninth and Fifth."

"Right." Although it was impossible, Jo could almost *hear* him grinning from ear to ear. "At twelve thirty."

Jo slammed down the phone without saying goodbye.

Irrationally, it flashed through Jo's mind that Janet was going to fire her on the spot, because Jo had just made a lunch date with Roarke. Jo was trembling as she hurried into Janet's office.

Janet was sitting behind her desk, drumming her

fingers noisily on the wooden surface. Her face was crimson with anger, her lips clamped shut in a thin straight line.

She couldn't be this angry because of a lunch date, Jo thought weakly to herself. Janet stared silently at Jo for several moments. It was so quiet in Janet's office that Jo could hear Janet's watch ticking.

"I'll bet you'll never guess who just called." Janet's lips barely moved as she spoke.

Jo shook her head helplessly.

"I'll give you three clues." Janet held up three fingers. "It was a co-worker of yours." She unbent one finger with her other hand. "She's not at work today because she says she's got the flu." Janet unbent another finger. "And, most interesting of all, she was totally confused by my compliments on the copy for the *Finlandia* brochure." Janet pointed all three fingers at Jo.

For a moment, Jo was so relieved Janet wasn't angry about Roarke that she didn't focus on the seriousness of the problem concerning Dacey.

"What I'd like to know," Janet continued, "is what the hell is going on around here. If it wasn't Dacey, then who wrote the damned copy?"

There was nothing to do but to admit that she'd written the piece. "I did," Jo whispered.

"But how did you know enough about the book to write the copy? When did you read the manuscript?"

"I read it the night I took the book home to paginate it."

"I see." Janet nodded. "That was certainly ambitious of you, Joanna. But why didn't you give Dacey the writing assignment yesterday, as I instructed?"

Jo didn't know what to say. She couldn't tell Janet that

Dacey had left early last night without getting Dacey in trouble and confessing she'd lied.

Janet sighed. "Listen, Joanna, I want to get to the bottom of this. You needn't look at me so mournfully, I'm not going to fire you." Janet's voice was considerably lower than it was a few minutes ago.

"Just answer this question: Did you deliberately keep the job for yourself so you could prove you were a better writer than Dacey?"

Stunned by the accusation, Jo could feel scalding tears of frustration welling up in the corners of her eyes. She fought to control her emotions. "Mrs. Tarlin, I'd never do anything like that. I couldn't find Dacey last night. She must've worked very late in Copyediting." Jo wrung her hands behind her back. "Anyway, I left without telling her about the assignment. When I got home I tried to reach her on the phone but she never answered. I knew how important the job was to you so I wrote the copy myself. I was going to give it to Dacey to rewrite but she never showed up this morning.

"I'm sorry if I did something wrong. I was only trying to help." Jo felt calmer after releasing this torrent of words. She'd managed to tell the truth (well, almost) and still cover for Dacey.

Janet waved her hand in a gesture of exasperation. "I don't know who to believe. As you can well imagine, Dacey is quite upset and I can't say I blame her. You really should have found her before you left the office last night, Joanna. You know how I feel about my people leaving early," she glared accusingly at Jo.

"However," she sighed, "the main thing is that the copy got written and, I must say, you did an excellent job for your first assignment."

Jo smiled hopefully at the compliment.

"Just for the record, Jo, eventually I would have given you the chance to prove your writing talents. Believe me, if you're as good a writer as I suspect, you'll be doing plenty of copy for me.

"But you must remember that in order to succeed here, or in any business, you've got to trust your co-workers. And your boss," Janet added, not unkindly.

Janet straightened up in her chair as if she were embarrassed by her honesty. "Next time I ask you who wrote something," she added sternly, "I'll expect an honest answer."

Jo nodded weakly, suppressing her frustration. She wished she could tell Janet everything and prove her innocence, but she knew she was trapped in her own lie.

"All right then. Let's forget the whole mess." Janet stood up. "Why don't you go to lunch; it's after twelve o'clock," she said, dismissing Jo with a nod of her head.

Jo turned quickly, suppressing an urge to slam Janet's door as she left the corner office, and walked back to her desk.

With her hip, Jo pushed her open drawer shut as hard as she could. The loud noise of the drawer slamming closed caused several people to turn and stare curiously at Jo. Someone giggled softly.

Jo tossed her head defiantly and grabbed her coat. She rushed out of the office to meet Roarke.

Luckily, Jo was able to flag down a cab directly outside the office. Climbing into the back seat, she told the driver her destination and sank into the lumpy cushions.

"What an incredible morning!" she muttered, shaking her head in frustration.

The cabby shot a glance in his rear-view mirror. He

caught Jo's eye and shrugged as if he were used to hearing passengers talk to themselves.

Jo ignored him. It's all Dacey's fault, she thought to herself. I covered for her and got myself in trouble.

To make matters even worse, Dacey will probably be furious with me, Jo thought miserably. Jo tried to take comfort by reminding herself that at least she had covered for Dacey's early departure from work.

Suddenly, all thoughts of Dacey evaporated. As the cab turned on Fifty-ninth Street, Jo recognized Murphy standing on the far corner. He was talking to a beautiful red-haired woman. The woman was much shorter than Roarke and he leaned over her as he gestured excitedly.

Jo asked the cab driver to stop immediately and let her off in the middle of the street. She paid the fare and got out of the cab without taking her eyes off Roarke. She was so engrossed in watching him that she forgot to tip the cabby. The driver angrily gunned the engine and roared away from the curb.

Roarke turned at the sound of the screeching cab. Instantly, he spotted Jo standing on the curb. He smiled, vigorously waving his arm at her.

Jo flicked a limp wrist in Roarke's direction.

He bent and kissed the redhead on her forehead. Jo's heart clutched in her chest as a pang of jealousy swept through her. She wanted to turn away but she couldn't take her eyes off the couple.

After patting the woman's cheek affectionately and saying a few last words to her, Roarke turned and ran towards Jo.

"Hi, love," he yelled, weaving through traffic to get to her side. Before she could turn her face away from him, he kissed her lightly on the cheek, the same way he'd kissed the redhead.

He hooked Jo's slender arm through his and pointed her towards Central Park. "I thought we'd have lunch in the Park today," he said excitedly.

"In the Park? Roarke, are you crazy? It's going to snow any minute." She stopped walking and stared at him, her eyes radiating light like a fine-cut emerald.

"Oh, come on Joanna. Where's your sense of adventure? You're from Vermont! You should love the snow." His enthusiasm was so infectious that Jo had to agree to the picnic.

"She's very attractive," Jo commented as they walked up Fifth Avenue.

"Who?" Murphy asked, bewildered.

She shot a glance at him, but he seemed genuinely confused by her remark. "The redhead," Jo said impatiently. "The woman you were just talking to?"

"Doris?" He elongated the name into two distinct syllables. "You think she's attractive?"

Jo nodded.

"Oh, well, to each his own." He shrugged. "She wears far too much make-up for my taste. The only way I recognize her in the office is by that red hair. Did you ever see such a color?" He chuckled, dismissing the subject of Doris with a shrug as they approached the entrance to Central Park.

Roarke led Jo down a graveled bridle path and deep into the park. They walked until they reached a small embankment with a view of a frozen pond.

Roarke unfastened the knapsack he'd been carrying on his back. He unpacked a thick woolen blanket and spread it under a huge willow tree.

Jo sat down, leaning against the tree trunk while Roarke dropped a quarter wheel of brie, a loaf of French bread, a bunch of grapes, and a bottle of wine on the blanket. He even extracted two wine glasses from his knapsack.

"I have to admit, it's very beautiful here," she said, tucking her legs underneath her for warmth. Luckily, she'd worn heavy wool pants and a fisherman's sweater to work that day.

"Only in New York could you sit under a willow tree and have your choice of watching skyscrapers or ice skaters." He paused, staring out over the snow-covered fields. "This hill is a special place for me. I discovered it several years ago, when I first came to New York. I come here quite often, but usually alone. You're probably the first person I've ever brought here."

"Why me?" she asked, fishing for a compliment.

"I guess because all the other women preferred eating at The Four Seasons," he joked.

It was not the answer she'd expected. Her lips puckered into a childlike pout.

Laughing, he leaned over and kissed her lightly on the cheek. "Darling, that was a compliment," he said as he opened the wine bottle with a small corkscrew.

He poured them each a glass of wine. "Now I'd like to propose a toast to our new living arrangement." He handed her a set of keys. "And a toast to friendly neighbors."

Jo smiled as they clinked glasses. She inspected the key ring. "Why are there two mailbox keys on this ring?" she asked, pointing to a pair of tiny keys.

"Oh, this one opens my mailbox." He pointed to the

darker key. "I'll be out of town till Tuesday so I was hoping you'd collect my mail for me."

"Sure. No problem," she said. "Are you going any place special?" She tossed the key ring into her pocketbook.

"No." He broke off a chunk of bread. "It's business. Nothing important," he said offhandedly. Obviously, he didn't want to tell Jo where he was going. Jo wondered if his trip included the redhead. Even though he'd dismissed her with a casual remark, Jo was having a difficult time suppressing the jealousy that she felt.

He scooped a dollop of cheese onto the piece of crusty bread and held it out for her.

Annoyed by his secrecy, she ignored the piece of bread he offered her. What kind of game was he playing?

Roarke shrugged as he popped the bread into his mouth. "Not hungry?" he asked.

Jo shook her head. "I seem to have lost my appetite," she said sullenly. She took a long swallow of wine.

"Hey! Go easy on the wine," Roarke warned. "As I recall, you have a pretty low tolerance for alcohol." He grinned.

Jo was not amused by his reference to the other night. Defiantly, she gulped down the remains of her glass and, reaching for the wine bottle, she refilled her glass.

"Jo, what's wrong with you today? Did something happen at the office this morning?" he asked.

"Nothing's wrong," she lied, avoiding his confused gaze. She stubbornly refused to confide in him. Why should she? He obviously didn't trust her. He'd avoided telling her about his morning meeting with Janet. And now this Doris. What kind of relationship did he have with *her?* The question brought tears of frustration to her eyes.

Roarke shook his head in confusion. "Jo, can't I help in some way?" he asked.

"No," she said, rubbing her eyes with the palms of her hands.

He ignored the cold tone of her voice as he leaned over and put his arm around her shoulders. He hugged her closely to him.

For a moment, Jo leaned into his chest, resting her head on his shoulder. But then she pulled away from him, denying herself the comfort of his support. She would show him she was just as independent as he was.

Roarke sighed loudly, removing his arm from her shoulder. "Well, I'm certainly not going to beg you to talk to me," he said. He began gathering up the food and utensils, packing them into his knapsack. "We may as well forget about this picnic." He glanced sideways at Jo, waiting for her reaction to his last remark.

Jo gulped down the remaining wine in her glass. She hesitated to say anything to him that would reveal her suspicions. After all, they'd only known each other for a few days. What right did she have to be jealous? Although she longed to reveal her inner turmoil, she stubbornly forced herself to remain aloof.

Roarke continued to stare intensely at her. Then he leaned over and, using considerable physical force, he pulled her into his arms.

He wrapped both arms around her and held her so tightly that she could barely breathe. His dark eyes flickered with light and Jo gasped, panicked by the intensity of his gaze. Suddenly, his lips came down on hers. She struggled to push him away but he would not release her.

His mouth covered hers; his warm breath seemed to breathe fire into her. She could feel his tongue against hers as he gently forced apart her teeth. She felt a quickening deep within her as she responded involuntarily to his embrace. Instinctively, she realized she was powerless to resist his sensuous explorations of her mouth.

Her struggling ceased. Overwhelmed by passion, Jo pressed herself into Roarke's arms; barely aware of how much she was encouraging him. Her hands flew to his face; then her fingers touched his thick, coppery hair.

A husky moan escaped from Roarke's throat. Holding Jo even closer, cradling her in his arms, his lips moved away from her mouth. Roughly, as if annoyed by her bulky clothing, he pulled at the neckline of her sweater, his lips impatient to caress the soft downy skin at the base of her neck. As his mouth pressed against her tender flesh, Jo's fingers tightened like a clamp around his head. She pulled his head closer to her body with a kind of urgency that she'd never before known.

His hands swept the length of her body. Jo could feel his fingers, chilly from the winter air, against her burning skin as his hands worked their way under her sweater. He squeezed her naked flesh and Jo felt a spasm of desire quake through her body.

Jo felt as though she were physically melting into his embrace. From somewhere along the bridle path, she could hear the galloping thunder of a racing horse and the pounding was matched only by her wildly beating heart.

Jo heard the not-too-distant voices of the horseback

riders. One of them giggled nervously as they sped by Jo and Roarke. The untimely interruption jerked Joanna back to reality. Mortified at being seen in Roarke's arms by strangers and, more importantly, frightened by the way she'd responded to Roarke's advances, she pulled her body away from him. "Roarke," she cried, "let me go. People are watching."

"I don't care who's watching," he growled. "I want to know why you're acting this way."

"I'll act any way I please," she said as she struggled to release his hold on her.

"Joanna, don't you understand?" He shook her gently. "I care about you and I want us to be close," he said softly.

She stopped struggling and stared into his coal black eyes. "Then why don't you trust me, Murphy? How can we be close if you insist upon cloaking everything in secrecy?"

"What are you talking about?" he demanded, releasing her. Quickly, she scrambled to her feet, brushing leaves from her pants. He stood up and held her flailing arms. "What have I kept secret?" he demanded.

Jo couldn't tell if he was feigning innocence or if he was genuinely confused by her accusation. "For one thing, your meeting with Janet yesterday," she said with a toss of her head. "You didn't tell me Janet was coming to your apartment in the morning. But you made sure I left by nine o'clock, didn't you?" For a moment, Jo felt that she'd gone too far, revealed too much. But it was too late to stop the flow of her bottled-up doubts.

"What are you and Janet trying to hide?" she demanded.

"Ah, so that's what this outburst is all about. Jealousy." He shook his head in disgust, turning away from Jo to stare at the skaters on the frozen pond.

Furious at his patronizing response and ashamed of herself for revealing her vulnerability, Jo spun around and ran down the bridle path. She had only gone a few yards when Roarke caught her arm and turned her around so that she faced him.

"You're acting like a child," he said. "And I'm sure that once you've had a chance to calm down, you'll regret this little outburst."

Jo tried to jerk her arm out of his hand but his fingers were clamped securely around her elbow. His words infuriated her, even though she knew he was probably correct. "What do you care how I act?" she demanded defiantly. "Why don't you just go off on your little business trip and leave me alone?"

"I don't think you want to be left alone, Miss Davenport. I think that's why you're so upset."

His remark shook what little confidence she had left. Were her feelings that apparent?

For a moment they stood staring at each other. Then Roarke released her arm, checking his watch at the same time. He led Jo down the gravel path to the street. Silently, they walked out of the park.

"I've got to run," he said as casually as if they'd been discussing the weather. "I'll see you when I get back. Janet and I are meeting in her office on Tuesday afternoon. If you're in the mood, maybe we'll walk home from work together."

Again, his attitude astounded her. Did he expect her to be waiting breathlessly for him to return to New York? "You are the most insufferable, arrogant man I've ever met!" Jo blurted out.

Although she truly meant to insult him, he took the remark as a joke. "Now, now, Joanna, flattery will get you nowhere with me."

He raised his hand to flag a passing cab. "Have a nice weekend," he said as a cab pulled up to the curb. "I hope your move goes smoothly."

"I may not take the apartment after all," Jo said with as much nonchalance as she could muster.

Roarke merely shrugged as he entered the cab. "Suit yourself," he said. "But that apartment's got to be the best bargain in Manhattan." He slammed the cab door closed and, with a grin on his face, he waved to Jo as the cab pulled away from the curb.

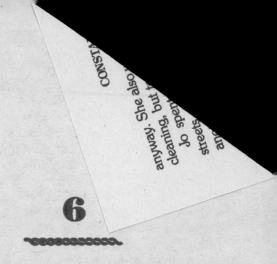

6

On Saturday morning Jo moved into her tiny studio on Carmine Street. She'd spent the past twenty-four hours debating whether or not to take the apartment, but logic had finally won out. Although she was disturbed by Roarke's arrogant attitude, he was right about one thing: this place was the best bargain in New York.

Jo had made up her mind that, for the time being, she would live there, but as soon as another place came along, she'd move out—as far away from Roarke as possible.

Jo had few belongings—everything fit neatly into two suitcases and a shopping bag—so the move required only one cab ride downtown. The cab driver helped carry her suitcases up the stairs.

The apartment looked the same as it had on the night Murphy had shown it to her. Even though the rooms were clean, Jo scrubbed the kitchen and the bathroom washed the windows. Usually Jo hated oday she enjoyed the tasks at hand.

t most of the weekend roaming the snowy of the Village. In the Village, she discovered ther side of city living. Compared to the intimidating glass skyscrapers surrounding Jo's uptown "hotel for women" the Village felt comfortable. People on the streets dressed casually and moved a little more freely than they did on the Upper East Side. Something about the Village reminded Jo of Falls Creek, and the comforting comparison made her feel at home.

Naturally, whenever she entered her new building from the street, Jo had to pass Roarke's apartment. She felt a twinge when she climbed the stairs in front of his door. Was she a fool to think she could keep her distance from Roarke once he returned from his trip? Would the sight of his front door always disturb her?

Refusing to give in to her fears, Jo kept as busy as possible all weekend. She found a twenty-four-hour grocery and shopped there several times. By Sunday evening, her cabinets overflowed with canned goods.

Monday morning Jo checked Roarke's mailbox, as promised, and piled the accumulated letters on her mantelpiece. Then she hurried uptown to work.

Monday was a hectic day at the office. Dacey was still out with the flu and, although Jo had twice her normal amount of work, she wasn't at all unhappy about Dacey's absence. She assumed that Dacey would be angry at her for having written the brochure copy of *Finlandia*.

In any case, Jo was too busy on Monday to spend time thinking about Dacey. The sales conference in Puerto Rico was only two days away and everyone in the office was frantically preparing for it.

In addition, Janet instructed Jo to organize an office party for Tuesday night for Roarke. Janet was throwing the party to celebrate the completion of *Finlandia*. Roarke's book had gone into Copyediting that morning.

Jo had to call and invite all the people on Janet's guest list. She also had to order the food and wine and run out on her lunch hour to buy cocktail napkins and plastic cups. By the end of the day, Jo was exhausted and her neck ached from clutching the telephone to her ear all afternoon.

When she got home from work Monday night, Jo took a long hot bath and was fast asleep by nine o'clock.

The next morning, Tuesday, Jo spent an hour getting dressed for work. She told herself she merely wanted to look as good as possible for Janet's party; Roarke's expected attendance had nothing to do with how she dressed that morning.

Unfortunately, there wasn't much to choose from in her closet. She'd worn her green "interview" suit so many times that it seemed dated to her by now. And her navy skirt and white sweater only reminded her of her dinner date with Roarke.

The only outfit left for her to wear was her lilac angora sweater dress. Jo's mother had hand-knit the knee-length turtleneck for the few times Jo had needed an evening outfit in Falls Creek. Jo loved the dress but, as she had been reminded each time she'd worn it, the tight-fitting sweater clung seductively to her slender body. Jo wondered if the dress was appropriate for the office.

At 8:30 Jo sat on her bed holding the green suit in one hand and the lilac dress in the other. She was angry and frustrated with herself for wasting so much time debating what to wear. With a disgusted flick of her wrist, she threw down the suit and put on the dress.

By 9:30 Jo suspected that the angora dress was a mistake. Janet teased her about "dressing formally for a little office party." The mailboy whistled under his breath every time he passed Jo's desk. Two of her fellow secretaries asked whom she was dating that evening (and if he had a friend). The only person who didn't have a comment was Dacey.

From the moment Dacey arrived at the office that morning, she completely ignored Jo. When Jo had timidly said "Good morning," Dacey had given her an icy stare and turned away. All day, Dacey sat at her desk with her back to Jo.

Jo quickly adapted to the situation. She worked around Dacey, never trying to talk to her again. When Jo had a question Dacey could easily have answered, she deliberately went to someone else for the information. In one day, she introduced herself to three new people in the company.

Janet was pleased with the work Jo completed that afternoon. She thanked Jo for helping her with the preparations for the sales conference. (Jo had typed Janet's speeches and verified the numerous dates of author tours for all of Janet's upcoming books.) By 4:30 Janet had everything she needed for Puerto Rico. She cheerfully instructed Jo to set up for the party.

Before she did anything about the party, Jo ran to the ladies' room to check her outfit and repair her makeup for the fifth time that day. All day she had worried about ruining her dress with a leaky pen or spilled coffee. Luckily, she'd come through the day intact. Even though she had taken a lot of ribbing about her dress, by the end of the day, Jo was pleased that she had worn it for the party. She took one last look at herself in the mirror, straightened her navy leather wrap belt and hurried back to the office.

At her desk, Jo hid all her papers and replaced her work with half-gallon wine bottles and plastic cups. Then she unwrapped the caterers' platters of cheese and crackers and opened several packages of paper plates and napkins.

A few people arrived early for the party. They had a quick drink at Jo's desk, awkwardly complained about train schedules or traffic, and then left the party before the guest of honor showed up.

By 5:30 the party was in full swing. Janet's office was crowded with elegantly dressed people. Expensive leather briefcases were piled high in the corner of the room. Empty wine glasses and dirty ashtrays covered every available tabletop. Judging by the noise level in the office, the party seemed to be going successfully.

Jo stood off to one side of the hallway. She didn't know many of the people who had arrived. Her peers in the "secretarial pool" hadn't been invited. Dacey was having an animated conversation with the author Clayton Downes, and Janet had cornered a book club editor from New Jersey.

Nervously, Jo checked her watch. It was almost six o'clock, and Roarke still hadn't arrived. Was he going to miss his own party?

Jo walked back to her desk and poured herself another glass of wine. Suddenly, from the corner of her eye, she spotted a flash of copper-streaked hair. She turned quickly and saw Murphy Roarke walking down the hall.

Roarke moved reluctantly, with hesitation in his usually

easy gait. His forehead was gnarled into a frown. Clearly, he was not particularly anxious to attend this party. He looked tired, as if he'd been working long hours. In his hand he carried a leather flight bag.

"Murphy Roarke! So you finally decided to grace us with your presence!" Janet shouted from the doorway to her office. Several people stopped talking and turned to stare at Roarke.

Murphy glared at Janet, his lips pressed tightly together. From the disgusted look in his eyes, Jo feared he might turn around and leave the party at that moment.

Janet's face froze for a second. Then she smiled rigidly and walked quickly down the hall, her heels clicking on the floor. "Oh, for heaven's sake, Murphy! Put your suitcase down and have a drink with us." She squeezed his arm affectionately. "Everyone here wants to congratulate you on finishing your wonderful book."

A well-dressed gentleman standing near Janet extended his hand toward Roarke. "Let me be the first," he said formally. "Congratulations, Mr. Roarke. I read *The Finlandia Affair* last night, and I think it's going to be a very big seller. A first-rate job!"

Janet beamed, turning to face Roarke.

Roarke was hardly listening to the gentleman; his eyes scanned the room in every direction but Janet's.

Janet poked Roarke's shoulder playfully. "Murph, you do remember Mr. Harris, don't you?"

Roarke turned and mumbled something to the older man.

Jo couldn't hear Murphy's reply. Suddenly, it seemed as though everyone at the party was talking at once. A group of people converged on Roarke, and his face disappeared into the crowd of well-wishers.

Jo took a long swallow of wine and discreetly wiped her lips with a cocktail napkin. She placed her empty wine glass on her desk. But then she didn't know what to do with her hands, so she picked up the glass and refilled it for the third time.

Then, suddenly, Roarke was at her side. She turned to him. Their eyes locked together for a moment, jade meeting onyx.

Up close, Jo could see tiny lines of exhaustion in the corners of Roarke's eyes. She had to suppress a sudden urge to soothe away the creases with tender strokes and loving kisses. She had to remind herself that she was still furious with him, even though his presence made her forget what they'd been fighting about in the first place.

Roarke reached over to touch a wisp of her sunlit hair, but Jo moved away from him.

"Hello, Murphy," Jo said, somewhat formally. "Would you like a glass of wine?" She reached for a glass on her desk.

He nodded his head. The tense muscles in his jaw relaxed into an easy grin as he helped Jo lift the heavy wine bottle. At the same moment, someone thrust an empty glass under the neck of the bottle.

Jo looked up. A thin man with a handlebar mustache stood next to Roarke, his glass extended midair for a refill. Murphy obliged by filling the glass with wine.

"Thanks, Murph, my man." The ends of the man's long mustache twitched as he grinned at Roarke.

Roarke looked at him in surprise. "Have we met before?" Roarke asked, perplexed.

The man shook his head vigorously and clapped Roarke on the shoulder. "I'm Bill Anthony," he said as if his name were a household word. "I'm a literary agent."

"Oh, you're Clayton Downes's agent," Jo exclaimed, recognizing the name from Janet's correspondence.

"That's right, pretty lady," he said, smiling broadly. "And who are you?"

"Jo Davenport. I work for Janet Tarlin."

"You're an editor?" Bill asked.

"No, just a secretary," Jo replied.

"I see," Bill said, his smile fading slightly. He turned to Roarke. "Well, it's fantastic to meet you," Bill said, excluding Jo from the compliment. Obviously, he didn't waste his flattery on secretaries.

"Likewise," Roarke said, politely nodding his head as he turned away from the flamboyant agent.

"Hey! Don't go away, man. Listen, this is no chance encounter. I've hung around New York for the past two days so I could speak to you at this party."

"Whatever for?" Roarke asked.

"For *Finlandia*, of course. I want it for the movies."

Roarke laughed. "How in the world do you know you want it? No one's even read it yet. I only finished the book last week."

"I don't have to read it." Bill pointed a finger at Roarke. "If you wrote it, it's good enough for me and my client. I represent a very big Hollywood producer who's interested in turning *Finlandia* into a box office smash," Bill said with confidence. "Sell us the rights, Murph, and we'll all make pots of money."

"No, I don't think so," Roarke said slowly. "So far I've resisted selling my books to Hollywood, and there's no reason to change my mind right now."

"Man, are you crazy? Do you have any idea how much bread there is in movieland?" Bill gestured emphatically with his hands.

Roarke shook his head. "No, and I really don't want to find out. Please, don't tempt me. But thanks for the offer anyway."

"You're making a big mistake, Murphy." Bill shook his head. "But, if you change your mind, just call me." Bill extracted a tiny leather case from his pocket. "Here's my card." He handed Roarke an engraved card from the case. "As I said, I can make you a very rich man."

Roarke stuffed the card in his pocket and nodded at Bill. Then, taking Jo's elbow, Roarke led her into an empty corner of the room.

"It's like a zoo in here tonight," he breathed into her ear. "Who invited all these people?"

"Janet. She says these people can help with your book," Jo explained. "I think she wants you to be nice to them."

"All of them?" he asked helplessly. "But there's only one of me and there's so many of *them*."

Jo pressed her fingers to her lips, suppressing a giggle. She felt very lightheaded from the three glasses of wine. "Come on, Roarke, be serious," she said.

Roarke rolled his eyes toward the ceiling and groaned. "Be serious she tells me." He waved his hand. "Everyone here is so serious they give me the willies." He shook his head. "They talk about the sales conference as if it were the presidential election."

"But Janet says the conference is really important for your book," Jo said.

Roarke laughed. "The sales conference is just an excuse for these people to lie in the sun, drink piña coladas, and flirt with each other."

"You've been to a sales conference?" Jo asked.

Roarke sipped his drink and nodded. "Once," he said.

"Janet asked me to come down one year and discuss my book with the salesmen."

"Was it fun?"

He laughed. "No, I'd hardly say it was 'fun.' The salesmen were very nice, and everyone was extremely enthusiastic about my book, but it was very hard work to be friendly to so many people for so many days. After the first day, the strain started to show on everyone. Cocktail hour got earlier and earlier as the days passed."

"Why aren't you going this year?" Jo asked, grateful that they had such an impersonal subject to discuss. Roarke acted as though their fight last week had never happened, and that was fine with Jo. "*Finlandia* is certainly the biggest book you've ever written."

"One sales conference was quite enough for me, thank you. I decided after the first trip that I was a writer and not a salesman. I leave marketing to the experts. And I'd like to leave this party in the hands of these expert guests." He was leaning so close to Jo that she could feel his warm breath on her cheek. "When do you think we could politely leave?"

"Roarke, you just got here," she scolded.

"I know. That was my first mistake," he said. "Except, of course, I knew you'd be here. If I hadn't seen your face I would never have put down my suitcase." He lightly touched her cheek and ran a finger down the side of her neck. She shivered involuntarily from his featherlight touch.

With a smile, he took a step back from Jo. His eyes swept down to her feet and then back up to her face. "Your dress is beautiful," he said. He raised his hand and touched her turtleneck collar. "I like the way this wool feels on the skin," he murmured. "And I especially like the way it hugs your body."

She felt a crimson heat race to her cheeks.

"I knew that compliment would make you blush," he teased.

Self-consciously, she avoided his intense gaze.

"So, what did you decide to do about the apartment?" he asked casually.

Jo twirled her wineglass. "I decided to take it," she said finally. "It is a great bargain."

"Yes, indeed. A *great* bargain." Roarke teased, his coal black eyes twinkling.

Jo tried to ignore the comment. "I moved in on Saturday. Oh, and I collected your mail, as requested."

"Stacks of perfumed fan mail, I suppose."

"No, but the gas company and New York Telephone still love you," she retorted.

The tension between them seemed to dissolve as they laughed together.

He pointed a finger at her. "We have a date to walk home tonight. Remember?"

Before Jo could answer, Janet appeared from behind Roarke. "A date to walk home?" she said loudly. "I haven't heard that expression since high school." Janet's hollow laughter echoed in Jo's ear.

"You're absolutely right, Janet," Roarke said angrily. "It does sound childish. For a moment I forgot we were at a sophisticated New York publishing party." He grabbed Jo's hand and nudged her down the hall. "Jo and I have a limo waiting outside to drive us home; I hope you'll excuse us, Janet. Thanks for everything; it was a lovely party."

"Wait a minute, Murph." Janet lunged to grab Roarke's arm. "Don't go yet. At least let's get some mileage out of all this wine and cheese," she whispered hoarsely in his ear. "Just come meet the book reviewer from the *New York Times.*"

"Janet, I've met the book reviewer from the *Times* six times. In fact I've met all the reviewers and book club editors in this room half a dozen times."

Janet squinted her eyes. "And you're a very successful author, Murphy Roarke." Janet barely moved her lips as she spoke.

"I'm a successful author because of the books I've written, Janet, not because of the parties you've given," Roarke replied evenly.

Janet blinked. "Of course, Murphy, I wasn't implying otherwise. . . ." Her hands fluttered around her wineglass and she nervously chewed her lower lip. "I guess you must be tired after your trip. You run along and I'll take care of the guests." She kissed Roarke lightly on the cheek and then turned to Jo.

"I'll be on my way to Kennedy Airport after the party, Jo. I'll be in Puerto Rico until next Monday. You have the phone number at my hotel but please don't call me unless it's absolutely urgent."

"Okay," Jo said. "Don't worry about the office; we'll take care of everything here."

"Yes, I'm sure you will, my dear." Janet's voice was saccharine. "As I recall, you live uptown, don't you Jo? In a hotel for women if I'm not mistaken?"

Janet's question was so unexpected that Jo didn't know what to say. She could feel her stomach lurch suddenly. "Yes, I did until this weekend. I just moved into a studio in the Village."

"Well, congratulations!" Janet patted Jo's shoulder. "Apartments are hard to come by in that part of town." Janet drained her wineglass. "I've spent a lot of time in the Village. What street do you live on?"

Jo cleared her throat. She glanced at Roarke before answering Janet's question. "Actually," she said slowly, "I'm living in Murphy's building."

"Murphy's building? On Carmine Street?" Janet turned to Roarke.

He smiled evenly at Janet as if he were vaguely amused.

"How convenient, my dear," Janet said. The comment was obviously meant for Jo, but Janet continued to stare at Roarke.

No one spoke for a moment.

"Convenient for whom?" Roarke asked.

"Why, convenient for me, of course. Convenient for me," Janet repeated. "Now Jo can deliver my memos to you, Murph." Janet raised her drink toward Roarke and a little wine sloshed out of the glass.

Roarke's fingers tightened like a vise on Jo's arm. She could feel the tension mounting in his body. She held her breath in nervous anticipation of what would happen next.

"Get your things, Jo," Roarke said. "We're leaving." He gently pushed her towards the coatrack near the wall.

When Jo turned to grab her coat, she noticed that Dacey had been standing directly behind Janet, eavesdropping.

Roarke and Janet didn't seem to be aware of Dacey or anyone else in the room as they stood glaring at each other.

Jo walked over to her desk to retrieve her purse from

the drawer. She was too far away to hear what Janet was saying to Roarke, but she did notice the possessive way Janet patted Roarke's arm as she spoke.

Roarke didn't answer Janet, he just continued staring icily at her.

"I'm ready," Jo said meekly as she returned to Roarke's side with her coat draped over her arm.

Roarke nodded at Jo and then turned to Janet. "Let's forget the whole thing, Janet," he said. "But just for the record, don't worry about your memos getting delivered. Since we finished the book last week, there shouldn't be any more memos between us." He spoke evenly yet emphatically.

Janet's jaw clamped shut.

Jo looked helplessly from Roarke to Janet. Then Roarke grabbed her elbow and walked her down the hall.

As they rounded the corner into the reception area, Jo turned her head to glance back at Janet and Dacey. The two women stood staring in Jo's direction. Then, with a smile, Dacey raised her wineglass and silently toasted Jo's departure.

As Jo watched, Dacey put her arm around Janet's shoulder and slowly led her into an empty office.

7

Outside the office building, Roarke took Jo's hand and led her uptown on Sixth Avenue. Wondering why they were headed uptown, Jo turned to question Roarke's direction but decided to keep quiet when she noticed the angry frown in his forehead.

He was staring straight ahead, his jaw firmly clamped shut. Jo had to walk very fast to keep up with Roarke's brisk pace.

At Fifty-ninth Street, Roarke turned right and they walked down Central Park South until they reached Fifth Avenue. To her surprise, Roarke led Jo through the shiny brass doors and into the lobby of the Plaza Hotel. They quickly walked over to the entrance to the Oak Room, one of the hotel's elegant restaurants.

In a few moments, the head waiter seated Jo and Murphy at a small table near the huge front windows overlooking the entrance to Central Park where several horse-drawn carriages, available for hire, lined Fifty-ninth Street.

Jo's face was flushed from the brisk walk and the warmth in the bar. She held her cold hands to her cheeks as Roarke ordered two brandies "to get rid of the chill."

Jo smiled nervously. Ever since they'd left the party in Janet's office, Jo had been fighting the fear that had unsettled her stomach when Janet had asked about Jo's new apartment. Jo realized unhappily that she was treading on thin ice with her boss.

Clearly, Janet was very upset about Jo's friendship with Roarke. Tonight, something had ignited Janet's temper, and Jo feared her job at Harris House was now jeopardized because of Roarke.

Roarke seemed to be reading Jo's mind. He gently took her hand and enfolded it in his as if he wanted to soothe away her fears. "Jo," he said softly, "I'm really sorry you got stuck in the middle of my feud with Janet."

Jo squeezed Roarke's hand, silently encouraging him to continue.

He rubbed his forehead wearily with his other hand. "Janet and I go through this every time we finish working on a book."

Jo felt a tightness in her throat and she swallowed with difficulty. To Jo, it sounded as if Janet and Roarke must have an ongoing, rather intimate relationship if Roarke could chart its ups and downs. Slowly, Jo pulled her hand out of his. With her finger, she traced the rim of her brandy glass.

"Murphy," she said shyly. "Could you please explain Janet's behavior tonight? If I'm going to get fired for moving into your building, I'd like to know why." She tried to sound like she was kidding, hiding her trembling hands in her lap. Jo realized she was forcing Roarke to discuss his relationship with Janet and, frankly, she was afraid to hear his response.

"Yes, I suppose you're right." Roarke sighed. "But it's difficult to explain." He sipped his brandy thoughtfully before continuing. "You see, Janet and I have a very close working relationship. After you edit a book that's important to you, Jo, you'll understand what I mean. But, for now anyway, let me try to explain it like this . . ." Again he paused for a few moments.

Jo wished he would get on with it. His long explanation was extremely nerve-racking.

"You see, good books work because people bring their personal perceptions to the written page. Some writers feel that finishing a book is a lot like giving birth to a child. It's an effort of love requiring a lot of hard work. But, in the end, the results are worth the effort. Somewhere in the process, you gain a tiny touch of immortality. At least you think you do."

He shrugged. "The analogy may be an exaggeration. I don't mean to trivialize anything. I just mean that when people work together creatively, they share a lot of emotional stress which brings them together in an almost intimate way."

"Almost intimate?"

Roarke grinned at the quizzical expression in Jo's eyes. "Yeah," he said with a laugh. "Almost, but not quite. Look, Jo, Janet has helped me with three books. She's given me hours of her time and expertise whenever I needed someone to discuss my work with. I trust her editorial opinion implicitly. Unfortunately, I have a hard time trusting people, especially about my work," he admitted.

"The problem is that once the book is written and sent to Copyediting, I'm finished with it. I'm anxious to get on with my next project. But Janet's work is just beginning, she's got to stay enthusiastic about *Finlandia* for months while she sells the book for Harris House.

"I think she starts to resent my detachment from the project. Invariably, we wind up fighting over something trivial. We've been through this with every book we've published together.

"I don't mean to ramble, Jo. Am I making any sense at all to you?"

Jo nodded. It all sounded plausible to her. However, she felt compelled to clarify one point, just to be sure.

"Yes," she said, nodding slowly. "You're telling me that the only thing between you and Janet is a working relationship, right?"

"Of course that's what I'm saying." Roarke shook his head. "Our personalities are certainly not compatible enough for an intimate relationship," he added.

Jo had to admit to herself that, as lovers, Janet and Murphy were certainly mismatched. "That's true," Jo said softly. "It's just that Janet acts as though she's your wife or something."

"More like my mother than my wife," Roarke corrected her. "But you're quite right about her possessiveness. Frankly, I don't know what to do about it. Janet's such a damn good editor. When I'm in the middle of my plotline and I can't figure out what to do with one of my characters, I can call Janet at two o'clock in the morning and she'll be interested in the problem. I can talk to Janet as if all the characters in the book were real people. At those times, I'm very grateful for her concern. But as soon as we finish the editing, we lose that connection, along with our patience with each other. And I start wondering if I'll ever be able to work with her again.

"I don't want to hurt Janet or cause her problems professionally, but I can't seem to control my impatience with her anymore. I suppose I'll have to find another editor sooner or later."

"Oh no," said Jo. "Your books are too important. If Janet is such a help, you'll just have to figure out a way to work with her."

At first Roarke seemed surprised, but then a warm smile spread across his mouth. "You've changed a lot since our picnic last week and I'm delighted with the results," he said, taking her hand again.

She shyly returned the smile. "And I suppose," she sighed, "I'll have to figure out a way to deal with her also. I do have a feeling my job is in jeopardy after this evening."

"Oh, I doubt it," Roarke said confidently. "I think that great success is waiting right around the corner for you at Harris House."

"Really? What makes you so sure?" Jo asked, perplexed by the self-assurance in his tone.

"Call it a gut feeling: the masculine version of women's intuition," he joked. "It never fails me.

"Besides," he added. "If anything goes wrong at work, you don't have to worry. I'd be happy to support you in the style to which you are not yet accustomed."

Jo was speechless, overcome by the implications of Roarke's offer. It was close enough to a proposal to inspire a lot of fantasies. Yet he spoke so flippantly that she wondered whether it was wise to take him seriously.

Jo's thoughts were momentarily interrupted by the waiter, who came by the table and handed the check to Roarke. While Roarke paid the bill and they gathered up their belongings, Jo fought to regain her composure.

By the time they were seated in a cab and speeding down Fifth Avenue, Jo started to doubt that she'd heard Roarke correctly. He acted as though they'd merely had a friendly drink and nothing extraordinary had been said.

When they arrived at Carmine Street, Roarke paid the fare, ran up the front steps, and unlocked the door to the brownstone.

Roarke followed Jo up the stairs to her apartment. He stood by the steps while she unlocked her door.

Then she turned to face him. "Would you like to come in for a cup of coffee?" she asked.

"Sure," he said simply. "I'd love to."

Inside her apartment, Jo's green suit lay crumbled on the floor next to her bed, a sloppy reminder of the trouble she'd had getting dressed this morning. With an embarrassed shrug, she quickly picked up the suit and hung it in her closet. Then, removing her coat, she hurried into her tiny kitchen.

Roarke stood in the middle of the apartment and surveyed the room. "The apartment looks great," he said with enthusiasm.

"Thanks," Jo replied, filling the coffee pot with water. She stood at the entrance to the kitchen and pointed to the fireplace. "You'll find your mail on the mantelpiece," she said.

Roarke nodded as he grabbed the pile of letters and

quickly thumbed through the mail. He stuffed two envelopes in his pocket and tossed the rest of the pile into the fireplace. "How about a fire?" he asked.

Jo nodded eagerly in approval of the suggestion.

Retrieving a few logs from the stack of firewood in the hallway, Roarke built a blazing fire in no time.

Jo carried a tray of cups to the table near the marble fireplace. "I was wondering who stored their wood in the hallway," she said.

"It's mine," he said. "I store wood all over this building. Use it whenever you like."

Jo poured a cup of steaming coffee. "Thank you," she said. It was hard for Jo to keep the somewhat formal tone from her voice. She realized that her conversation with Roarke had become stilted from the moment they had entered her apartment. It was curiously exciting and, at the same time, unsettling to be alone with Roarke in her own home.

Roarke held a spoon to his coffee cup. "Do you have any more sugar?" he asked, pointing to the empty sugar bowl.

"Sorry," Jo replied, quickly jumping up and rushing into the kitchen. "I'm sure I bought a bag of sugar this weekend."

Opening her cabinets, Jo saw the sugar on the top shelf. On Sunday, she had used a chair to reach the high shelf, but now she didn't want to bother moving the chair from the other room. So, she stretched on tiptoe and reached for the sugar.

Her fingers barely touched the bag when a sudden pain ripped across her shoulder blades. She gasped loudly and quickly lowered her arm.

Roarke raced into the kitchen. "What on earth happened?" he asked, his voice full of concern.

"It's nothing," Jo lied. "I must've pulled a muscle or something in my arm. The sugar's up there, can you reach it?" She pointed to the top shelf but another pain in her shoulder caused her arm to fall limply by her side.

"Forget the sugar," Roarke said impatiently. "Let me look at your arm." He led her into the living room and sat her down on a chair.

Gingerly, his fingers prodded her upper arm and the muscles across her back. She winced when he applied pressure to her right shoulder blade.

"Um," he murmured thoughtfully. "That's the spot." Gently, he began massaging her shoulders.

Although his touch was gentle, Roarke had tremendous strength in his fingers as he kneaded Jo's shoulders. Slowly, Jo felt her tense muscles relaxing and the pain soon subsided. She closed her eyes and luxuriated in the sensation of Roarke's powerful hands on her back.

He stood behind her as he continued to massage her shoulders. Then his fingers moved up her long neck and he gently massaged her temples. Unconsciously, Jo moaned as the soothing sensation relieved the tension in her neck. She felt as if she were floating weightlessly.

As Roarke rubbed her forehead, Jo could feel her hair slip out of its French knot, but she didn't have the energy or the inclination to fix it. Soon, her long golden hair cascaded loosely down her back.

Roarke grabbed a handful of her silken hair and stroked it between his fingers. He walked around the chair and stood facing Jo, still caressing a handful of her hair through his fingers.

"Why do you always pin up your hair?" he asked.

She shrugged, surprised at the question. "I don't know," she said. "It's just easier to wear it up I guess."

"But it's so beautiful," Roarke whispered, almost to himself. "I've never seen a color like this before."

In the glowing firelight, Jo's hair was shot through with streaks of platinum. Roarke continued to twirl the long strands between his fingers as if he couldn't believe it was real.

Kneeling before her, he closed his eyes slowly as he pressed a lock of her hair to his lips. Then he gazed up at her. His dark, languid eyes were full of longing as he searched her face. He seemed to be waiting for a sign from her.

Unwavering, Jo steadily returned his gaze. It seemed to Jo as though an unspoken question had been asked and answered. She was not afraid but, at the same time, she could barely breathe in anticipation of what would happen next.

Shyly, Jo reached over and stroked his cheek. Her fingertips lightly grazed the rough beginnings of a slight stubbly beard. She wondered what his cheek would feel like if it were pressed against her skin and the thought made her shiver.

Roarke pressed forward and leaned closer to Jo. She could feel his warm breath on her neck. Very tenderly, he lightly kissed her lips. Then he stood and, gently holding her arms, he pulled her to her feet. Her body was so relaxed from her massage that she swayed into his arms.

His chest felt like a rock against her as she involuntarily pressed the weight of her body into his. She breathed in his rich, masculine smell and felt her legs weaken. She felt as though she were sinking into the floor and had to hold onto Roarke in order to keep her balance. She leaned deeper into his embrace.

His hands swept up and held her face. He kissed her eyelids, then her cheeks and, finally, her full, satiny lips.

His kisses were like nothing she'd ever known. His lips seemed to burn into hers, and from deep within her a warmth like heated brandy began to flow through her veins. She longed for him to hold her even closer.

Ever so slowly, his hands moved away from her face and down her back. His arms hugged her body with the same gentle mixture of power and passion she had felt when he'd massaged her back. Only now, his fingers lingered as if he were touching her skin instead of her soft woolen dress.

His hands moved to her waist and encircled her for a moment. Then he slid his fingers around to the front of her body. A deep moan escaped from his throat as he tenderly stroked the valley between her firm, ample breasts.

Her nipples hardened instantly and Jo was astonished by the mixed ecstasy of pain and pleasure. For the first time in her life, Jo felt consumed by an overwhelming physical longing. Instinctively, she knew that Roarke was the only person in the world who could possibly satisfy the primitive passions that raged within her.

Folding his arms around her, Roarke lifted Jo off the floor and carried her across the room. The sudden movement sent Jo's head spinning and the dizzying sensation melted into all the other new physical sensations she was experiencing. She had no choice but to give in to the emotions she was feeling.

"Jo, my darling," Roarke said in a husky whisper as he gently lowered her onto the bed. "I want you so much."

Roarke's remark triggered a reflex in the pit of her stomach. She wanted to tell him that she felt the same way, but she couldn't speak. However, her trembling body seemed to reveal to Roarke that his desires were matched.

He responded by kissing her more and more intensely and the fire within Jo blazed through every fiber of her body.

Soon they were sprawled across her bed, their bodies entwined in a passionate embrace. Jo lost all sense of time and place. For the moment, Roarke was the only thing that existed in her universe. More than anything else, Jo wanted to please him.

But she didn't know how to return the exquisite pleasure he was giving her.

"Show me what to do," she blurted out.

"What?" he asked, sounding slightly befuddled.

"Show me what to do," she repeated, her cheeks burning with embarrassment. "I don't know how to make you . . . happy."

"You've already made me happy," he said softly as he hugged her. "Darling, there are no rules. Do whatever feels right and it *will* be right."

She nodded wordlessly, suddenly understanding the meaning of his words. He leaned over and kissed the hollow at the base of her neck.

His kiss was like fire and she could no longer bear the weight of her wool dress on her burning skin. She stood up quickly and unbuckled her belt, dropping it on the floor with a low thud.

Roarke was startled by the sudden movement. Then a slow smile spread across his face. He reached down and grabbed the hem of her dress. Very slowly, he lifted the dress over her head and dropped it over the bedpost.

Jo stood before him clad only in her beige camisole.

His eyes swept down over her half-naked body. She could almost *feel* his eyes on her, and the sensation filled her with longing. She reached over and slowly started unbuttoning his shirt.

After releasing the final button, Jo began caressing his muscular chest. She kissed his naked shoulder and he moaned with pleasure.

Astonished by her own aggressive behavior, Jo was nonetheless thrilled by the desire in Roarke's voice. Gaining ever more courage from his passionate responses, she boldly continued undressing him until he lay naked and glistening with sweat on the bed. She ran her hands down the length of his body.

Suddenly Roarke rolled off the bed and onto his feet, pulling Jo with him. His hands were shaking as he slipped the narrow straps of Jo's camisole off her shoulders. The lacy undergarment tickled Jo's skin as it floated to the floor. With her hands on his shoulders, Jo stepped out of the garment.

Wrapping his arms around her waist, Roarke drew her to him and buried his face in her breasts. He kissed her flat tummy before his hands tugged at the waistband of her pantyhose. Gently, he removed the hose while his mouth continued exploring her exposed flesh.

He flung her hose across the room and she stood before him completely undressed. She shivered from both the cool air and the thrill of desire that ignited every nerve-ending in her body. Roarke pulled her toward him and they tumbled together onto the bed.

For a moment, she lay on top of him but they quickly rolled over so that Jo felt the weight of his muscular body pressed against hers. She no longer wondered what to do next; she wrapped her arms and legs around him, guided by sheer instinct.

Jo had never imagined such joy. She was consumed by a thousand new sensations of longing and ecstasy. She felt as if her body was moving outside of her control. She held tightly to Roarke as if her life depended on being as close to him as possible.

Jo belonged to Roarke at that moment and nothing in the world could stop the flood of passion sweeping through her. Only Roarke seemed capable of extinguishing the fire raging within her. She abandoned herself to him and, in the release of her restraint, she experienced a physical satisfaction such as she'd never believed possible.

Much later, Jo lay quietly in Roarke's arms. He tenderly stroked her hair and his gentle caresses lulled her into a dreamless sleep.

When she awoke the next morning, Roarke's arms still held her lightly. She was surprised to discover that he was wide awake and staring at her. They snuggled closely in the small bed.

He kissed her forehead and yawned loudly.

"Have you been awake for a long time?" she asked.

"Um," he murmured sleepily. "Not too long, but I've had enough time to watch you sleep for a while."

Jo laughed to hide her embarrassment. Somehow the act of watching her sleep when she was totally vulnerable seemed more intimate than making love. "I hope I didn't embarrass myself in my sleep. I mean, I wasn't snoring or anything, was I?" She giggled nervously.

"On the contrary," he said seriously. "You're very beautiful when you sleep." He hugged her for a moment. "And I have you all to myself," he added.

Roarke laughed at the rosy glow that came to Jo's cheeks. He seemed to enjoy her awkward moments. She frowned and he kissed her happily on the cheek. Then, sitting up in bed, he grabbed her hand. "Come on, lazybones, I've waited long enough for you to get up. We've both got a busy day today and I'm starving. Let's get showered."

"Okay." Jo grinned. "You go shower first and I'll start breakfast."

"No way," he said. "Let's shower together."

"Together?" Jo gasped. She'd never showered with a man in her life.

"Of course together," Roarke said as he pulled her out of the bed.

In vain, Jo tried to cover herself with the blanket from the bed. Roarke tugged the blanket from her clenched fists. "Joanna, you have a gorgeous body. I won't let you hide it from me," he said with determination.

It was a request Jo found difficult to refuse after last night. With a helpless shrug, she abandoned the blanket and followed Roarke into the bathroom.

Roarke stepped into the shower and turned on the hot water. A cloud of steam began to rise above the shower curtain.

Jo pinned up her hair with a long barrette. She hesitated a moment before following Roarke into the shower.

He grinned as she stepped over the edge of the tub. "Don't be afraid. I don't bite," he joked, baring his teeth. He leaned over and lightly sank his teeth into Jo's shoulder.

She pulled away from him. "Hey! You said you don't bite," she laughed, rubbing the red spot where he'd nipped her.

"So, I lied." He shrugged.

"Oh, you!" Jo reached up and pushed his head under the shower, instantly soaking Roarke's hair.

He grinned. "Don't play rough with me," he warned. "And now that you've gotten my hair all wet, you can just wash it for me." He grabbed a bottle of shampoo from the ledge of the tub and handed it to Jo.

Nodding her consent, she squeezed a dab of shampoo into her hand. "At least you could bend down," she commanded, "so I can reach." He did as requested and Jo lathered his thick head of hair.

Meanwhile, Roarke grabbed a bar of soap and rubbed it against Jo's arms. Then he moved the soap up her shoulders. She could barely concentrate on the simple task of washing his hair as his fingers traveled down her throat and covered her full breasts. He massaged the soap into her flesh until her nipples were erect and her fair skin flushed with rosy color.

His hands moved down her waist as Roarke continued to cover Jo's body with thick suds. His fingers probed her fleshy inner thighs, and Jo could feel her knees almost buckle underneath her. She was quite overwhelmed by the sensuous soaping.

Roarke leaned over and quickly rinsed the soap out of his hair. As water flowed down his back, Jo soaped his athletic shoulders and his lower back. He murmured contentedly as she continued massaging his thick muscles.

He turned and drew Jo into his arms. "You'll have to get closer so we can both fit under the shower." His mouth covered hers and he kissed her with great hunger and longing.

Jo sank into his embrace, melding her mouth to his. Their bodies were slick with soap as they pressed together under the steamy flow of water.

Suddenly, the water temperature dropped radically and they were shocked by a splash of cold water. Jo squealed as she jumped out of the shower.

"Damn boiler," Roarke growled to himself as he turned off the water. He grabbed a towel and quickly dried himself. Then he took Jo's towel away from her and dried her back with a few brisk strokes.

"Lucky thing that water doused us," he said; "or we'd have been in the shower all morning."

Jo was too shy to reveal how disappointed she was that their embrace had been halted by the cold water. She'd never imagined that a shower could be so intimate and exciting.

Jo slipped into her terry bathrobe and Roarke draped a towel around his waist. They hurried over to the kitchen.

"I'm absolutely starving," Roarke said as he extracted eggs, milk, bread, and bacon from the refrigerator. "I want two helpings of everything—eggs, juice, toast, jam, coffee. The works."

"My, my, it sounds like you haven't eaten for days," Jo said.

"I haven't," Roarke replied, matter-of-factly. "I was going to order a pizza last night but, somehow, I forgot all about it." He winked at her.

"I wonder why," Jo teased.

As she prepared breakfast, Jo marveled at how comfortable she felt with Roarke. It was almost as though waking up in his arms, showering together, and eating breakfast with him was an everyday routine for them.

Jo broke four eggs into a ceramic bowl. Smiling to herself, she marveled at Roarke's love-making of the night before. Jo had always feared that her first night with a man would be filled with awkwardness, embarrassment, perhaps even pain. But it had been nothing like that. Her lingering emotions involved passion, contentment and fulfillment. She innocently wondered if things would always be as wonderful with Roarke.

After they finished breakfast, Roarke stood up and strode over to the door. "I'll leave you to get dressed," he said. "Have a nice day at the office." He kissed her lightly on the cheek.

Jo felt somewhat disappointed by the way he casually left her apartment. She didn't quite know how she expected him to act; it just seemed that he could have made some reference to when they'd see each other again. If, in fact, he *wanted* to see her again.

A wave of insecurity washed over her and she admonished herself for being so immature. She was a big girl now and it was just plain silly to let her insecurities get the best of her. With an angry toss of her head, she forced herself to concentrate on getting dressed for work.

At the office, Jo quickly got to work logging-in the manuscripts accumulated in the wake of preparations for the sales conference. The morning was quiet since so many of the executives were in Puerto Rico, and Jo, like many of her co-workers, had a chance to catch up on a lot of work. She continued working steadily until she was interrupted by the ringing of Janet's phone.

"Hello. Janet Tarlin's office," Jo said.

"Hello," said a pleasant female voice. "May I speak to Joanna Davenport, please."

"Speaking."

"Hi, this is Doris Bower from the *Times*. I think you called me once about my boss, Misha Rakovich?"

"Oh, yes, Miss Bower," Jo said, excitedly hoping Misha was calling. "What can I do for you?"

"Actually, I'm calling to do something for you," Doris continued. "Misha got your letter the other day and he's agreed to publish his book with you."

Jo laughed happily in amazement. "You're kidding," she said and then instantly felt ridiculous. Why did she always say "you're kidding" whenever she was surprised about something?

Doris laughed. "Nope, I'm not kidding. In fact, I'm quite surprised myself. This morning Misha sent me a note to call and tell you to go ahead with the contract for the book. Since the columns belong to the *Times*, the contract will have to be between the paper and Harris House. I suppose we should let our lawyers battle out the financial arrangements."

"My boss will have to negotiate the contract with Misha's lawyers," Jo said.

"Of course, but Misha's agreed in principle to the idea for the book and that's what's important."

Jo's heart was pounding with excitement. "Are you sure about this?"

"Absolutely. I've had all of Misha's columns xeroxed

for you. I thought I'd drop them by your office this evening after work. Is five-thirty okay with you?"

"Fantastic. And thank you so much, Doris. I can't tell you how much I appreciate your help."

"Not at all, Joanna. Congratulations."

Jo felt like dancing around the office when she hung up the phone. She'd done it; she'd gotten Misha Rakovich for Janet.

Jo suddenly remembered that she'd never discussed her letter to Misha with Janet. Would Janet be upset that Jo had proceeded without her consent? More important-ly, would Janet approve of the idea of an anthology?

Without hesitating another moment, Jo picked up the phone and dialed Janet's hotel in Puerto Rico.

Janet had to be pulled out of a meeting to accept the call, and she was very abrupt with Jo when she said hello. But Janet's foul mood changed immediately when she heard Jo's reason for calling.

Janet was thrilled to add Misha to her list, and she loved the idea of an anthology. After getting the phone number of Misha's lawyer from Jo, Janet hung up.

About an hour later, Janet called back to tell Jo she'd worked out the preliminary details of a contract between Misha and Harris House. Janet felt that the book would sell better if it were published immediately. Her plan was to rush the project through production and publish it in the fall, along with Roarke's book. She asked Jo to start reading the columns right away and to make a rough compilation of the pieces that they would use in the book.

Janet was already planning her announcement to the sales conference when she hung up the phone.

Janet's enthusiastic response to Jo's call alleviated any fears Jo had about her position at Harris House. Janet never even mentioned the party or her argument with Roarke. Jo was amazed that everything had changed because of one little phone call.

She couldn't wait to share the news with Roarke. Forgetting his behavior that morning, she immediately dialed his apartment.

Roarke was pleasant on the phone, but he didn't seem at all surprised by the news of Misha's book.

"Jo, didn't I tell you that you were going to be a great success at Harris?" he asked.

"So, you're also a psychic?" She laughed. "Among your other numerous qualities."

After saying goodbye to Roarke, Jo spent the afternoon cleaning off all the work on her desk so that she'd be free to work on Misha's columns when Doris delivered them that evening. Jo planned on carefully reviewing every column to acquaint herself with Misha's work.

About five-thirty that evening, the receptionist called to inform Jo that Doris was waiting in the reception area. Jo hurried down the hall to meet her.

Jo had a wide smile on her face as she entered the reception area. The receptionist returned the smile and pointed to a slender woman who stood looking at herself in the wall-to-wall mirror.

The first thing Jo noticed about Doris was her bright red hair. The orangey color instantly reminded Jo of something Roarke had once said to her: "The only way I recognize her in the office is by that hair. Did you ever see such a color?"

Jo tried to recall when Roarke had said that. Then she remembered. She stopped walking and stood stock-still.

The redhead turned to face Jo.

Jo had seen Doris once before, about a week ago, on the day Jo met Roarke for a picnic lunch in Central Park. Doris was the woman Roarke had been talking to on the corner of Fifty-ninth and Fifth.

8

~~~~~~~~~~~

Jo stared at Doris in total disbelief.

Why hadn't Roarke told her Doris worked for the mysterious Misha Rakovich? What was Roarke trying to conceal?

With these questions rumbling around in her head, Jo was having a difficult time concentrating on her conversation with Doris. The two women were sitting on the couch in Janet's office, reviewing the stack of xeroxed columns in Doris's lap.

"Misha felt you should have everything," Doris said. "He's been writing a daily column for nearly three years so there's quite a lot for you to review. How many columns do you think you'll use for the anthology?" Doris asked.

"I don't know." Jo shrugged. "I suppose Janet will decide." Jo looked away from Doris; it was almost painful for her to be sitting here with the red-headed woman.

Doris shifted uncomfortably on the couch. "Well, give me a call as soon as you decide how many columns you'll need. And let me know if there's anything else I can do for you," Doris said, handing the pages to Jo.

Absent-mindedly, Jo thumbed through the stack of xeroxed pages. She nodded, staring at the floor.

Doris looked at her watch. "Oh, dear, it's almost six; I'd better run," Doris said as she stood up to leave.

Jo rose off the sofa to escort Doris out of the office and, for a moment, the two women stood staring at each other. Neither of them knew what to say next.

"Well, I'm sure I'll be talking to you on the phone soon." Doris extended her hand to Jo. "It was nice to meet you," she said.

"You, too," Jo replied, shaking Doris's hand without enthusiasm.

Doris turned and headed toward the door to Janet's office. She put her hand on the doorknob and then stopped. Slowly, she turned to face Jo.

"Jo, is there something bothering you?" Doris asked softly, chewing her lower lip.

"Why do you ask?" Jo said suspiciously.

"I don't know," Doris said. "You've been acting, well, peculiarly since we met in the lobby tonight." Doris shrugged. "I wondered if I'd said something to offend you." Doris's voice was genuinely concerned, and Jo suddenly felt terrible for having been so cold to her.

"Oh, no, Doris. Really, you've been wonderful," Jo said sincerely. "It's just that I was surprised when I saw you outside."

"Why?" Doris asked, perplexed.

Jo had no choice but to explain the situation to Doris. "Well, you see, I recognized you from last week."

"Last week?" Doris shook her head in confusion. "Jo, we've never met before."

"We've never been introduced. But I saw you on the street. You were talking to Murphy Roarke on Fifth Avenue. Roarke and I had a lunch date and . . ."

Doris snapped her fingers, interrupting Jo's explanation. "For a picnic in Central Park!" Doris laughed. "Of course I remember that day." Doris's smile was warm and friendly. "So, *you're* the special woman in Roarke's life," she said.

Jo felt a deep blush rising to her cheeks.

Doris was nodding her head knowingly. "Murphy was so excited that day. He kept talking about a wonderful young woman he'd just met. I swear he acted just like my seven-year-old son. I was amazed. Roarke had never talked about a woman before!" Doris shook her head in amused resignation. "That man!" she exclaimed.

It occurred to Jo that Doris discussed Roarke in the same motherly tone Janet sometimes used. Obviously, Roarke brought out the maternal instinct in a lot of women, Jo thought wryly to herself.

"Don't get me wrong," Doris continued rapidly. "I love Murphy like a brother, but all he ever talks about is business, business, business! He's still a young man. There should be more to his life than work."

"Well, I suppose business must occupy a great deal of Murphy's time," Jo said carefully. "How could he have any spare time for romance between writing books for us and columns for the *Times?*"

"Columns for the *Times?*" Doris repeated, her eyes widened in disbelief. "What do you mean?"

There was no backing down now, Jo thought to herself. "Doris, I think Murphy Roarke and Misha Rakovich are the same person," Jo said firmly. She crossed her arms over her chest and stared defiantly at Doris.

From the way her eyes slanted and the way she cocked her head, Doris looked like she was considering the possibility for the first time. She mulled over Jo's accusation.

Then she shrugged. "No, I don't think so," she said as if she were rejecting the idea completely. "I used to wonder about Misha's identity, but after all these years I've given up trying to figure it out.

"My impression, though, is that Misha's a close friend of Roarke. I think they live near each other, so Roarke picks up a lot of Misha's mail.

"Besides, I've always had the feeling Misha Rakovich is an older man. His writing is too rational to be the work of a thirty-five-year-old."

Doris pointed to the xeroxes on Janet's coffee table. "Read through those columns and tell me what you think."

With her arm extended, Doris suddenly noticed her watch again. "Oh dear," she said. "I really do have to run." Doris raced out the door and waved goodbye to Jo as she hurried down the hall.

Jo walked slowly back to Janet's office and sank down on the small couch. Her eyes were fixed on Misha's columns. The stack of xeroxes had to be eight inches high. Was a clue to Misha's identity buried somewhere in his columns?

Jo grabbed a handful of pages and relaxed back into the cushions of the couch.

Doris's words were ringing in her ears as Jo read through a dozen columns. It was true that Misha's writing displayed a certain maturity and an understanding of history that was unlike Roarke's work. Roarke's novels portrayed the world in a shotgun manner, scattering world events and political theories at random. In Roarke's books, politics served as a dramatic backdrop to a personalized search for self-discovery. In contrast, Misha's columns celebrated the old cliché that fact is stranger than fiction.

To Misha, history constantly repeated itself; to Roarke, history was everchanging. Jo concluded that Doris was correct; Misha's columns couldn't have been written by the same man who'd created *The Finlandia Affair.*

Jo pondered the dilemma all the way home on the subway. Roarke hadn't exactly lied to her, but he had concealed the fact he at least *knew* Misha Rakovich. How much influence had Roarke exerted to get Misha to publish a book with Harris House?

Jo walked down Carmine Street, debating whether or not to raise the topic with Roarke. As she passed by her brownstone, she peeked into Roarke's front window. His shades were up and, with his lamps blazing in the living room, Jo could see Murphy sitting at his desk. He was talking on the phone.

Suddenly, he turned and noticed her standing on the street. He waved and signaled her to come into his apartment.

Roarke was opening his apartment door as Jo entered the building. He rushed to her side and kissed her on the cheek.

"Hello, darling," he said affectionately.

"Hello," she said. Her stomach fluttered at the touch of his warm lips.

"You feel so cold," he said as he touched her cheek. "Come in and sit by the fire."

"In a minute," Jo said. "Let me just go upstairs and change my clothes." She started climbing the stairs, anxious to spend a few minutes alone before talking to Roarke; she needed to sort through her conversation with Doris and to think about the articles she'd just read.

"Sure," he said, somewhat confused by the faraway look in her eyes. "But hurry back."

She nodded and continued up the stairs.

"Hey!" Roarke called out when Jo reached the second floor landing.

She leaned over the railing.

"How about a pizza?" he called to her. "I'll call and order it while you change."

"Fine," Jo replied as she moved away from the stairs and unlocked her front door.

In her studio, Jo collapsed into a chair for a moment. She wondered how to handle the issue of Misha with Roarke. Jo was torn between appreciating Roarke's efforts on her behalf and feeling betrayed by the deceptive tactics he'd employed to help her.

With a sigh, Jo kicked off her shoes and started undressing. She changed into jeans and a sweatshirt.

In her bathroom, Jo splashed cold water on her face and stared at her reflection in the mirror. For several minutes, Jo considered unbraiding her hair. She vividly remembered Roarke's reaction last night when her hair fell loosely down her back. Although it would have been a small gesture to please him, Jo decided to leave her hair pinned up. Tonight she wanted to talk to Roarke, and letting her hair down might distract from the seriousness of the conversation.

Jo tossed her hand towel over the shower rack, grabbed her keys, and walked down the stairs to Roarke's apartment.

He opened his door immediately, obviously having been listening for the sound of her footsteps on the stairs.

"One double-anchovy pizza is on its way to Carmine Street," he proclaimed as Jo entered his apartment.

"How did you know I love anchovies?" she asked.

His face froze in disbelief. "Jo, I was kidding," he said slowly. "I'd never order double-anchovies. *Nobody* eats anchovies," he said. Then his forehead wrinkled. "Or do they?"

"They do. Trust me. A lot of people like anchovies." She patted his shoulder. "Especially me."

"Ah, well. Next time you'll get triple anchovies as compensation. Okay? Meanwhile, can I get you a drink?"

Jo nodded. "White wine, please."

Murphy went into the kitchen and Jo walked over to the fireplace. She rubbed her hands in front of the blazing fire.

Roarke called out from the kitchen. "I guess you had a pretty exciting day at work," he said.

"Yeah. I did." Jo was grateful that Roarke had raised the subject so quickly.

Balancing two full wine glasses, he walked into the living room. "You sounded so happy when you called me this afternoon." He handed the glass to Jo.

She sipped the wine, nodding her head at the same time. "Um. It was exciting. My first book, and all."

"Good," Roarke said. "I'm really happy for you." He looked at his watch. "But how come you're so late getting home? It's almost nine-thirty."

For a moment, Jo felt as if she were being cross-examined, but the concern in Roarke's eyes quickly melted her suspicions.

"Well, I stayed late at the office to read some of Misha's past columns." Jo walked over to the couch and sat down. She rested her wine glass on her knee. "A woman named Doris brought a stack of xeroxes to the offices." Jo avoided Murphy's dark eyes.

"Doris? Oh, you mean Doris Bower."

Jo nodded. "The redhead. You know her, of course," she said shyly.

"Doris?" Roarke smiled sheepishly. "I forgot about Doris."

"What did you forget?"

"That you noticed Doris the day we had lunch in Central Park." Roarke sank slowly into the couch.

Jo blinked. "I'm surprised you remember that meeting."

"Of course I do, Jo," he said disgustedly. "I remember every conversation we've had."

Jo was flattered by his last remark, but that still didn't explain Roarke's relationship with Misha Rakovich. She decided to confront the issue as openly as possible.

"Murphy, how do you know Doris?" Jo asked evenly.

Roarke sighed. "I met Doris through Misha," he said quietly.

Jo glared at him. "Then you do know Misha Rakovich?" She meant to sound casually detached, but her voice carried the sarcastic drawl of an accusation.

"Yes," Roarke admitted. "I know him very well."

"But why didn't you tell me?" Jo said with a cry in her voice.

"Jo, I couldn't. I promised Misha."

"I don't quite understand the reason for all this secrecy," Jo said sarcastically.

Roarke shrugged helplessly. "Misha claims he needs his privacy; he insists on it. Misha's columns make him a very powerful man in New York. His opinion influences a lot of people and his voice is heard daily by millions of people. He doesn't take his responsibility lightly and I respect his wishes. He feels that if he doesn't reserve a certain piece of himself for himself exclusively, he'll always be in jeopardy of mistrusting his own judgment."

"How could he jeopardize his own judgment?"

"It's easy in New York. This is a very seductive city, Jo, and you have to be careful about people here. This is not Falls Creek, where you've known your neighbor since third grade. You simply can't trust too many people in this town."

"I think you're politely saying that you didn't trust me," Jo said miserably.

"No," Roarke replied emphatically. "Not you. I've always trusted you. But I don't particularly trust the women you work with. Janet would go to any lengths to publish a book by Misha." Roarke shook his head for emphasis. "Including firing you if she felt it would help."

"Or promoting me if I got Misha for her?" Jo questioned.

"Yes," Roarke said. "That's why you went out and got him."

"I know," she whispered. "But I wanted to do it on my own."

"Jo, you did it on your own. The anthology idea was yours, and you must have written a very convincing letter to Misha. I may have influenced him a little, but I certainly couldn't have ordered him to do anything he didn't want to do." Roarke laughed dryly. "Misha's hardly the type to be ordered around by anyone."

"But you kept saying that I would succeed at Harris House; you must have known Misha would accept my offer," Jo said, crossing her arms over her chest.

"Joanna, I knew you would succeed because you're bright and you care about your work. If it hadn't been Misha's book, it would've been some other book. I simply feel that you're destined to succeed in any job you undertake."

"I appreciate your encouragement," Jo said, "but I really wanted to succeed on my own."

"You will. Or you won't succeed at all. No matter how much influence you use, it only goes so far. Ultimately, you always succeed on your own hard work and effort." He took a short swallow of wine.

"Sure, as long as I get a lot of help from my friends." Jo knew she was prolonging the point longer than necessary. She wasn't really mad at Roarke for influencing Misha; she just resented the way he had handled the situation. She stubbornly wished Roarke had confided in her from the first.

"What's wrong with a little help from your friends? It was okay for the Beatles," he joked.

His flippancy infuriated her. "Why did you do this for me, Murphy?" She spat without thinking about what she was saying. "What do you want in return?"

Murphy's dark eyes narrowed in anger. He slammed his wine glass on the coffee table and the delicate glass tinkled as if it might shatter. "Jo, I hope you didn't mean that last remark," he said menacingly. His face was like granite.

Jo swallowed hard to prevent herself from crying. Confused and miserable, she didn't understand how the conversation had come to this. "No, I didn't," she said softly, staring at the carpet.

He turned towards her and raised her head with his fingertips. "Listen Jo, I was only trying to help. What's wrong with that? Why can't you accept my help as a gesture of friendship? You might give me the benefit of the doubt by remembering that I trusted you enough to recommend you to Misha. Please don't go looking for ulterior motives in everyone or you'll wind up like Dacey," he said.

"Heaven forbid," Jo laughed.

Roarke reached over and took Jo's wineglass from her hand and placed it on the coffee table. Then he moved closer to her on the couch.

He wrapped his arms around her body and hugged her tightly to his chest. She sank into his arms, greedy for the comfort of his warm embrace.

His head bent over hers and he planted tiny kisses on her neck. Involuntarily, her shoulder flexed as a shiver tickled her neck.

Shyly, Jo rubbed the collar of Roarke's shirt between her fingers.

He leaned over and his lips covered her mouth. She returned his passion in equal measure, her hands digging into his back to draw him closer to her.

Suddenly, the doorbell chimed and they were both jolted by the ringing. "Saved by the bell!" Roarke teased.

"So who wants to be saved?" Jo joked in her best Barbra Streisand imitation.

They laughed together as Roarke went to meet the delivery man at the door.

Roarke returned to the apartment holding a huge cardboard pizza box. He carried the box into the kitchen. Jo followed him and they stood staring at the pizza as if it were an unwanted intruder.

"You know, hot pizza always burns the roof of my mouth," Jo said.

Roarke grinned. "I know what you mean. Let's wait till it's good and cold before we eat it." He wrapped his arm around her shoulder and pointed her towards the bedroom. "It might take hours before it's cool enough," he warned.

"Um," Jo murmured, wrapping her arms around his neck. "What'll we do till then?"

He playfully nibbled her earlobe. "Well, we could always start the evening with dessert," he whispered huskily in her ear.

In response to his splendid suggestion, Jo kissed him affectionately. "Perfect," she declared.

Their pizza didn't get eaten until well past midnight.

The next morning, Roarke gave Jo a key to his apartment. He didn't offer a lengthy explanation when he put the key in her hand. "This may come in handy if I get locked out of my apartment," he said with a grin.

She nodded her head and smiled shyly. She couldn't speak because her throat was choked with emotion.

After that morning, Jo visited Roarke's apartment at least once a day. Most of the time she found Roarke working at his desk—on his next book, which he wouldn't discuss.

Jo used his key only once, on Monday, when she dropped off Roarke's mail from the office. She rang his bell several times but when he didn't answer the door, she let herself in with the key. Alone in his apartment, she laid the stack of mail on his desk. Several papers and opened letters were scattered across his desk. Jo fought the urge to sneak a peek at Roarke's new manuscript.

That night, Jo took a long hot bath. She lathered herself repeatedly with heavily scented suds. Where was Roarke, she wondered to herself? She tried to suppress a feeling of jealousy, but it was difficult.

Before she went to bed, Jo called Roarke's apartment and was relieved when he answered the phone. He said he'd been out with friends and asked if she wanted to come down to his apartment.

She was already in her nightgown, and she felt a little guilty for calling to check on his whereabouts so she declined his offer.

But, half an hour later, alone in bed and unable to sleep, she changed her mind. Throwing on a long robe and slippers, she ran down the stairs and, with her key, she unlocked his door.

Peeking through the passageway into his bedroom, Jo saw that Roarke was lying in bed, propped up on two pillows and watching television. He smiled when he saw Jo walking through the kitchen and into the bedroom. He flipped down the blanket and opened his arms. She slipped quietly into bed next to him.

He was watching a black-and-white Joan Crawford movie, and he started relating the story line to her but she was asleep before he finished. The touch of his body next to hers was all she needed to fall securely into a deep sleep.

At the office the next day, Janet returned from Puerto Rico looking tanned and relaxed. She greeted Jo warmly, asking about Jo's progress on Misha's book. She suggested that Jo have a drink with her after work.

Janet had a busy day catching up with her week-old correspondence and phone calls. Naturally, Jo worked as hard keeping up with her. By five o'clock Jo was exhausted.

Janet took Jo to The Four Seasons for a drink. The Four Seasons, one of the most chic restaurants in New York, was austerely decorated with dark charcoal-gray carpeting and black tables. But elegant floral arrangements softened the severe effect. Jo recognized two famous television personalities sitting around the free-floating bar.

They sat at a tiny table near the bar and ordered white wine spritzers.

"Now, tell me about your progress with Misha's book," Janet said. "Have you read through the columns yet?"

Jo smiled eagerly. "Most of them. You were right about Misha, he's an extraordinary writer."

Janet nodded. "I know. Have you thought about structuring the book? How should we divide the columns?"

Jo was pleased that Janet had asked for her opinion. "I thought perhaps we could classify the columns by topic. Economics, Politics, Foreign Affairs, and so forth," Jo said nervously.

Janet thought about the idea for a moment. "Yes, that makes sense. How many columns would you use?"

"I spoke with Eddie in production and we did some

arithmetic. If we shoot for a 356-page book, I figure we could easily reprint about 250 columns."

"Sounds like a respectable size to me. I'm impressed, Jo. You've really done your homework."

Jo beamed, delighted by Janet's compliment. "Thanks," she said. "Although I have to admit it doesn't really seem like work to me; I enjoy reading the columns so much."

"I know what you mean. Sometimes I feel that I would pay Harris House to let me work on my books." Janet leaned back in her chair. "Like Murphy's novels, for instance," she added casually.

Jo looked up quickly, uncertain about Janet's last comment. An uneasy silence settled between the two women.

"How is Murphy?" Janet said slowly. "I haven't spoken to him since our office party."

"Oh, he's fine," Jo said, avoiding Janet's intense gaze. "He's working hard on his next novel."

"Oh? What's this one about?" Janet asked.

"Frankly, I don't know. He doesn't want to discuss it with me."

"I'm surprised. I mean, I thought he'd take you into his confidence. You and Murphy seem pretty close."

"We are close," Jo said boldly, "but he's very secretive about his work. He says he'll only discuss it with his editor." Jo smiled warmly. She wanted Janet to know that she wouldn't interfere with Janet's working relationship with Roarke.

Janet's tense face relaxed into a friendly smile. "Authors are strange animals, you know," Janet said lightly.

"I know," Jo laughed. "But they're also very loyal.

Murphy always says you're the only editor he'd trust with his work."

Janet seemed pleased and embarrassed at the same time. "Thank you, Jo. That's very nice to hear." Janet fidgeted with her cocktail napkin.

"Jo, I think I owe you an apology for my rude behavior at the party," Janet said awkwardly. "Sometimes I'm just a witch, especially around sales conference time. Truthfully, I was also feeling a little threatened by your friendship with Murphy."

Janet raised her hand to prevent Jo from responding to her last remark. "You don't have to say anything, Jo. Just accept my apology and we'll leave it at that."

"There's no need for you to apologize, Janet. And, just for the record, you don't have to worry about losing Roarke. I've got a long way to go before I'm ready for an author of Roarke's stature. Meanwhile, I'm very grateful that I'm learning editing from a professional like yourself. I feel very fortunate to be working for you."

Jo was amazed at herself for being able to express herself so openly. She realized how much she'd learned about honesty in the past few weeks.

Janet responded warmly to Jo's sentiments. "Look, Jo, I can't go into details, but there are several administrative changes being planned. I think you will be very pleased with my plans for you."

Jo tried to get more details but Janet wouldn't reveal anything further. The only thing she added to the conversation was her promise to reward Jo for getting Misha's book.

By the time Jo and Janet left The Four Seasons, Jo felt they had reached a turning point in their relationship. Somehow they were closer than before, and Jo truly felt she had Janet's support both in terms of work and her relationship with Roarke. Janet had even suggested that Jo and Murphy have dinner one night at Janet's apartment.

During the cab ride downtown to Carmine Street Jo decided to celebrate the evening by buying a bottle of wine. She got out of the cab on the corner and stopped in the local wine store. Then she hurried down the street, extracting Roarke's key from her purse as she walked up the front steps.

As she opened Roarke's door, Jo heard a male voice coming from the kitchen. Although it wasn't Roarke's voice, it sounded vaguely familiar to Jo.

Roarke was sitting on the couch in the living room, and he got up as soon as he saw Jo. "Hi, love," he greeted her warmly. He hurried across the room to her side and kissed her lightly. Then he gently turned her towards his guest.

Jo was astonished to see Bill Anthony in Roarke's kitchen.

"Hello, Miss Davenport," Bill said enthusiastically. He raced to Jo's side and planted a kiss on each side of her face.

Jo nodded at him, offering a feeble greeting. She was terribly distraught at having used Roarke's key in front of Bill. What if he mentioned the incident to someone in the office? But there was nothing to do now except act as nonchalant as possible.

Jo handed the bottle of wine she'd just purchased to Roarke and, after taking off her coat, she sat down in the wingback chair. "Please don't let me interrupt your conversation," she said sweetly.

"Right." Bill clapped his hands together enthusiastically and then pointed to Roarke. "As I was saying, this is a bona fide offer. Say yes, Murph, and you'll have an advance check for one hundred thousand dollars in your hands tomorrow."

Roarke grinned. "I don't know, Bill," he replied good-humoredly. "It's certainly a lot of money; that's for sure."

"Man, this is only half of the advance. Once we're in production, you'll get the next fifty grand, and when the movie's released, your share will total two hundred grand. That's almost a quarter of a million dollars."

Jo's eyes widened in disbelief. "A quarter of a million dollars," she repeated breathlessly.

Bill laughed loudly. "Only the tip of the iceberg," he enthused. "There's more money if Roarke wants to write the script and, with the points we're offering, he could be a millionaire if the picture takes off in the provinces."

"Points?" Jo asked.

"A percentage of the profits," Roarke explained to Jo. "Similar to book royalties."

Bill chuckled again. "Show me a book that pays these kinds of royalties," he said dramatically.

Roarke laughed with him. "Yes, you're right about that." He turned to Jo. "I can make more money selling *Finlandia* to Hollywood than I've made publishing three books." He turned back to Bill. "I told you not to tempt me, Bill," he added.

"Couldn't help it, man. This producer friend of mine laid this offer on me and I just had to fly with it. So, come on, Murph, whaddya say? Should I have my girl draw up the papers?"

"Whoa!" Roarke exclaimed, holding up his hand. "At least give me a chance to discuss it with Jo."

Bill looked surprised, but he recovered quickly.

"Sure, Murphy, anything you say." He picked up his coat. "You two discuss it, and I'll call you later."

Bill made an elaborate procedure of kissing Jo and pumping Roarke's hand as he said his farewells. "I told you I could make you a rich man, Murph. Just give me the go-ahead and you're on easy street. And think about writing the screenplay. You might like it better than writing novels; it's certainly more lucrative."

Roarke slowly closed the door behind Bill and turned to Jo. "So? What do you think?" he asked.

"Oh, Roarke, it's so much money!" Jo exclaimed.

"I know." He grinned. "Isn't Hollywood amazing?"

"What are you going to do?" Jo asked.

"I don't know." Roarke sat down on the couch. "I've never been offered this much money. It's awfully tempting." Roarke shook his head.

"What's your objection to selling your books to the movies?"

"It's hard to explain but, somehow, I've always felt I shouldn't make a lot of money from my work. I know it's crazy but I grew up thinking you made a choice in life. Either you worked for money or you worked for your art. It always seemed to me that true artists did better work when they were poverty-stricken." Roarke grinned sheepishly.

"Like Van Gogh," Jo said. "I read once that Van Gogh earned a total of two hundred and fifty dollars during his entire lifetime."

Roarke laughed. "Well, I wouldn't exactly put myself in a class with Vincent Van Gogh but, yes, the comparison is correct. I'm just afraid that if I make a great deal of money, no one will take my work seriously. Everyone will think I've sold out or something. Does that make any sense at all to you?"

"Yes, I understand what you're saying, but I don't necessarily agree with you. I think people will always take your work seriously because you take it seriously, and it shows," Jo said emphatically. "It doesn't matter if the movie flops, *The Finlandia Affair* will always be a great piece of literature."

"How do you know? Have you read it?" he asked with a twinkle in his eye.

"Yes, of course," Jo replied with a flirtatious grin. "I stayed up all night reading it. Why do you think I fell asleep on your couch that first night we had dinner?"

Roarke was laughing delightedly as he rushed to Jo's side and bear-hugged her to his chest.

"That's what I love about you." He laughed. "You always know exactly what to say." He kissed the top of her head.

She fairly glowed with joy at his words. Although spoken casually, his remark was almost like a real declaration of love. She warmly returned his hug.

"So, my darling, what shall we do with your Hollywood friend?"

"Your Hollywood friend," she corrected playfully. "No one is offering me a quarter of a million dollars. And my advice is that you should do whatever feels right," she added.

"You're what feels right," he said in a husky whisper. Then he raised her head with his fingertips. "Will you love me even if I'm a rich Hollywood screenwriter?" he asked. He was smiling so broadly that Jo couldn't tell whether or not he was teasing. Neither of them had ever mentioned love before.

Just then the phone rang. Roarke walked over to the desk and picked up the receiver.

"Hello," he said into the mouthpiece. "Bill," Roarke laughed. "Where are you calling from? Well, you must've *just* gotten back to your hotel." After a moment, Roarke nodded his head. "Yes, I've been discussing it with Jo."

Roarke looked at Jo as Bill continued talking on the other end of the phone. Jo could almost hear Bill's words as his voice reverberated in the receiver.

"One minute, Bill," Roarke said, placing his hand over the mouthpiece to the phone.

He looked at Jo. "You didn't answer my question," he said to her.

"I didn't think you were serious," Jo replied uncertainly.

"Jo! I've just put $200,000 on hold! Isn't that serious enough for you?"

She giggled. "Yes. Yes. I'll love you in spite of your bank account," she said happily.

Roarke smiled at Jo and nodded his head once. He removed his hand from the phone and raised the receiver to his ear. "Okay, Bill, draw up the papers." Roarke winked at Jo. "You've got yourself a deal."

9

Dear Mom," Jo wrote, "it's snowing like crazy today! According to the radio, this is the biggest snowstorm of the year. Everyone is complaining, but not me. I love New York in the snow; it reminds me of home.

"I can't believe six weeks have gone by since Murphy and I visited you for the holidays. We had such a lovely Christmas. Murphy says he gained five pounds from eating your sweet potato pie all weekend, but it was worth every ounce!

"I'm sorry I haven't written sooner, but I've been so busy. I'm working really hard on Misha's anthology, (Remember I told you about the book?) and I hope it will be ready for April publication.

"Murphy's book is also being published in April, and the advance reviews are very exciting. Looks like he's written another best-seller. I'll send you a copy as soon as I can.

"Murphy's been thinking about working on a screenplay for his book. He's been offered a lot of money for the project, even though he's never written a screenplay before. It would be a great opportunity for him, but it would also mean he'd have to move to the West Coast for a couple of months, so I have mixed feelings about the project. I'd miss him so much if he left New York.

"Oh well, I'm not going to think about that now. I'll be Scarlett O'Hara and think about it tomorrow.

"As I said before, everything at the office is going really well. My boss keeps promising me a big promotion and a raise in salary. I hope it's soon, so I can send you more money. Meanwhile, here's a check for $50. I hope it's enough for now.

"Take care of yourself, and I'll write again as soon as there's news about Murphy's movie."

Jo was addressing the envelope for her mother's letter when the phone rang.

Murphy was working at his desk in the living room and he ignored the phone, so Jo answered it in the bedroom. It was Bill Anthony and he wanted to speak to Roarke.

Jo called to Roarke, and he finally picked up the extension. He hated to be interrupted while he worked, but Bill had insisted on talking to him. Jo was certain their conversation had to do with Roarke's decision about writing the screenplay. She considered eavesdropping, but immediately rejected the idea and hung up the phone.

She finished addressing the letter to her mother and sealed the envelope. Then she got up off the bed and walked into the kitchen.

Jo could hear Roarke talking on the phone to Bill and

she lingered by the refrigerator, spending more time than necessary opening a can of diet soda. Unfortunately, she couldn't understand their conversation, as Bill seemed to be doing most of the talking.

Despite the cavalier attitude of her letter to her mother, Jo was worried sick about the prospect of Roarke moving to Los Angeles. Although he'd only be gone for a few months—she kept reminding herself—Jo knew it would be difficult to be separated from him.

In the past two months, Jo had spent almost every day with Roarke. For all intents and purposes, they were living together. She still paid rent on her apartment upstairs, but she rarely spent the whole evening there. It was virtually impossible for Jo to fall asleep at night if Roarke wasn't lying next to her.

Jo sighed as she went back to the bedroom. She lay down on the brass bed and picked up *Running Wild*, a manuscript she'd started reading the night before. It was a long romantic novel by an unpublished author that had arrived unsolicited at the office. On impulse—because she liked the title—Jo carried the novel home yesterday. She was enjoying the manuscript, but she couldn't concentrate and, after reading only a few pages, she tossed the novel on the bureau and decided to take a bath.

Jo quickly undressed and turned on the hot water. Pinning up her hair, she lowered herself into the bathtub.

Jo loved bathing in Roarke's eight-foot antique tub. She sank into the steaming water and felt her tense muscles relaxing. Luxuriating in the warmth of the water, Jo rolled a towel and used it as a pillow for her head.

Jo tried not to think about Roarke, but it was impossible. What will I do if he moves to L.A.? she wondered. The thought was so painful that it brought tears of self-pity to her eyes.

Suddenly, her solitude was interrupted by the sound of the bathroom door opening. Jo quickly splashed a handful of water on her face to conceal the tears in her eyes.

"Anyone around here need her back washed?" Roarke asked, grinning flirtatiously.

Jo raised her hand, mimicking a schoolgirl in class. "Me!"

Laughing, Roarke sat down on the edge of the tub and yanked up one sleeve of his sweater. He reached into the water, grabbed a bar of soap, and started sudsing Jo's back. His fingers dug deeply into her shoulder muscles and Jo moaned with pleasure as his strong hands massaged her back. Lately, Jo's body was plagued by various aches and pains; either she wasn't getting enough exercise or worrying about Roarke was putting her under severe physical strain.

"That was Bill on the phone," Roarke said quietly. He splashed warm water on her back.

"Yes, I know. What did he want?" Jo asked as casually as possible. Her arms were wrapped around her knees and she hugged her legs tightly in nervous anticipation of Roarke's response.

"He needed an answer from me," Roarke said. "About whether or not I wanted to write the screenplay," he added unnecessarily.

"What did you tell him?" she asked, staring at her toes underwater.

"Well, you know I'm having an awful time with this new novel. It just isn't going anywhere. So," Roarke sighed, "I told him I'd give the screenplay a try. Who knows? Maybe I'll get past my writer's block if I change projects."

Jo closed her eyes slowly. Her stomach lurched as if she were riding a rollercoaster. She concentrated all her energy on remaining calm. "So when will you be leaving for L.A.?" she asked.

Roarke dropped the soap in the tub. "Bill is sending us two airline tickets for next week," he said as he stood up. He grabbed a towel and dried his hands.

Jo turned slowly to look up at him. "Two tickets?" she breathed.

"I was hoping you'd come with me," he said simply.

"You really want me to come to California with you?" Jo asked, fishing for confirmation that she hadn't imagined his offer.

"Of course I want you with me. I wouldn't go without you." He smiled boyishly. "I sort of assumed you'd want to join me." He sat down again on the edge of the tub.

Jo couldn't believe her ears. He was so blasé about his invitation that Jo wondered if he were really serious. Would he tease her about something this important?

"What about my job?" Jo asked. "I just can't leave the office for a few months. Janet would have to replace me."

"Um," he said thoughtfully. "You're probably right about that. Oh well"—he shrugged—"maybe you'll find work in Los Angeles. Anyway, it won't matter much if you don't. I'll be earning a fortune for this movie deal," he said as if that explained everything.

"What does your salary have to do with me?" she said timidly.

"Dummy," he laughed. "I'm saying I'll take care of you; you don't have to worry about working anymore."

"Define 'taking care of me.' "

"Taking care of you. Four words. I'll put it in question form. Will you marry me?"

Jo's jaw dropped open. "You want to marry me?" she asked, dumbfounded.

"If that's the only way I'll get you on the plane," he joked.

Jo's hand flew to her mouth. "Oh Murphy," she cried quietly, her throat choked with emotion.

His face loomed above hers. The flippant twinkle in his eye was gone; he stared at her with serious intent. "My darling," he whispered. "I love you so much. Please say you'll marry me."

"Of course I will," she said excitedly. "I love you, Roarke." She threw her arms around him.

She grabbed him with such force that he slipped backwards and splashed, fully dressed, into the tub.

At first, Jo was mortified by what she'd done. She felt like a clumsy idiot.

For a moment, Roarke's mouth froze into a round circle of surprise. Then he exploded with laughter. *"This is the thanks I get for proposing!"* he roared. "A dunking!"

Jo burst into a fit of giggles. He looked ridiculous, his arms and legs askew in the narrow tub.

They couldn't stop laughing. Every time Roarke attempted to pull himself out of the tub, he'd slip and fall back into the water. Each attempt set off another gale of laughter.

Finally, he swung his legs up, around Jo, and he settled

lengthwise in the tub. "As long as I'm here, I might as well get clean," he said, grabbing the soap and lathering his jeans.

Jo's cheeks ached from laughing so hard. She'd never seen Roarke in such a clowning mood. Jo felt as though she would explode with happiness.

Finally, spent from laughter, Jo and Roarke sat in the tub shaking their heads and grinning at each other. For a long time, they sat looking at each other.

Then Roarke reached over and lightly passed the palm of his hand over Jo's shoulders. Her naked body glowed from the hot water. "Your skin feels like satin," he murmured.

He ran his fingers down her arm and raised her hand to his lips. Deliberately, he kissed each finger.

His sensuous kisses sent gooseflesh rippling over her torso. She raised her body a few inches and maneuvered her body so that she sat in his lap. Her back was towards him, and he wrapped his arms around her. She snuggled contentedly against him.

Roarke leaned over and kissed the back of her neck until she moaned with pleasure.

Then, twisting arms and legs in the narrow tub, Jo and Roarke managed to stand up.

Roarke held Jo's fragile shoulders and drew her to him. Holding her close, he kissed her roughly on the mouth. His mouth was warm and pleasurably wet against hers and Jo returned his passionate embrace.

Roarke's dark hair and clothes were dripping with water. He playfully shook himself like a shaggy dog and drops of water splattered over Jo. Begging him to stop, Jo tried to shield herself from the water but Roarke continued to splash her.

Jo felt as though she would burst with joy. He really wants to marry me, she kept repeating to herself. The thought filled her with a loving sense of security.

She shivered as the cool air hit her water-soaked body and Roarke draped a towel around her. He hugged the towel to her, rubbing the water off her body. Then he quickly stripped off his wet clothes.

She hung his jeans over the shower rack while he dried himself with a towel.

"I'm so sleepy," Roarke said with a mock yawn. "I'm going right to bed."

Jo giggled. "Me, too."

Holding hands, they raced into the bedroom and jumped into bed. Roarke pulled the down quilt over their bodies.

Under the quilt, they nestled together, entwining their arms and legs. For several minutes they hugged each other tightly, the warmth of their bodies gradually increasing with their mutual passion.

Roarke kissed her hungrily on the mouth. His lips seemed to devour hers during the long passionate kiss. Jo felt quite breathless by the time the kiss ended.

"I love you so much," she whispered.

"It's a good thing," he replied. "Because I'm about to ravish you from head to toe." He kissed her ear and his teeth gently nipped her earlobe. Then his mouth traveled slowly down her neck.

Lightly, he passed his lips over her breasts until her nipples rose like small, hard buds. He continued moving down her body until he'd reached her ankles and he turned and repeated the voyage.

He gently turned her over in the bed and, starting at the base of her neck, he planted kisses all along the length of her spine. He kissed her buttocks, her thighs, and her calves.

His kisses left Jo burning with desire. She felt as though a tidal wave of longing and desire were overpowering her. She closed her eyes and felt herself melt into the sensation.

Although Roarke was the only lover she'd ever known, Jo was certain that he was very different from most men. Roarke treated Jo as though she were the most precious woman he'd ever known and, in his arms, Jo really felt as though she was, indeed, very special.

Making love, they were like one body, moving together to a primitive rhythm known only to perfectly matched lovers. It was almost as if their hearts were beating in unison.

Later, snuggled against Roarke in bed, Jo relived his unconventional proposal and its humorous and then loving aftermath. She fell asleep dreaming about a flowing organza wedding dress and a huge bouquet of angel's breath flowers.

The next morning, Jo got up early to cook blueberry pancakes, Roarke's favorite breakfast. He was still sleeping soundly by the time the food was prepared, so Jo carried a breakfast tray into the bedroom.

Roarke was delighted by the breakfast-in-bed treat. He wolfed down the pancakes in short order.

Meanwhile, Jo was quickly getting dressed for work. She was much too excited to eat.

"Thanks for the pancakes, love," Roarke said as he wiped his mouth and tossed the napkin on the tray. He moved the tray to the empty side of the bed.

"I'm glad you liked them," she said as she hurried across the room to the bureau.

He grabbed her wrist as she passed the bed.

"Pancakes are my second favorite breakfast treat," he said.

"And what's your first?" she asked with a smile.

He pulled her arm so that she fell into his lap. "You," he whispered in her ear.

Jo laughed as she returned his kiss. After a few minutes, she reluctantly pulled herself away from him and finished dressing for work. Before she left the house, Roarke told her to start planning a wedding; they'd discuss the details that evening.

Jo was mentally making a guest list of her Falls Creek friends as she rode the subway to work that morning. But as the train neared the platform for her office, her thoughts shifted to problems at work.

In the past two months, Jo had really enjoyed riding the subway in the morning because she'd been excited about getting into the office and throwing herself into work. Her days had passed rapidly and, at night, she'd left the office feeling satisfied with the work she was doing.

That morning, Jo was thinking about writing a reader's report recommending *Running Wild* for publication, when she suddenly realized she had to confront Janet and quit her job. A part of her instantly regretted the decision. She'd be giving up Misha's book just when it was so close to completion. Also, there was *Running Wild* and two other projects she wanted to get published.

The more she thought about it, the more she had to admit to herself that she was hurt that Roarke took her career so lightly. Why hadn't it occurred to him that Jo might object to giving up her job?

Oh, she was certain she loved him, and marrying

Roarke was the culmination of her most cherished dream. But she wondered what would happen if Roarke hated Los Angeles. And, if Bill Anthony was an indication of the people they'd meet in California, surely they'd be coming back to New York. Then Jo would have given up her job for nothing. Could she afford to take that chance?

In her heart of hearts, Jo had to admit she felt that her career should be just as important to Roarke as his writing was to her.

It may not have been the world's most profound revelation, but it set Jo's head spinning. Only a few months ago, she would have given up everything to marry Roarke. Today she was filled with doubts and misgivings.

However, by the time Jo got to her desk, she had managed to put her confusion out of her mind. She wanted to marry Roarke and, at this point, one of them had to compromise. Jo was willing to give up her career if that was the only way to keep them together.

With a determined look in her jade eyes, Jo asked Janet if they could talk privately. When Janet tried to stall until that afternoon, Jo insisted upon an immediate meeting—she was afraid she would lose her courage if she had to wait.

With a sigh of impatience, Janet told Jo to come into her office.

She took two urgent phone calls before she finally turned her attention to Jo. "All right, Joanna. What is it that can't wait a few hours?" Janet asked.

Jo was startled by the abrupt tone of Janet's voice and she hesitated for a moment.

Janet quickly held up her hand as the phone rang

again. She answered it in a rush, asking the caller if she could return the call later in the day. Again Janet turned to Jo.

"I'm sorry, Jo. There's so much going on today, I'm really pressed for time." Janet quickly glanced at her watch. "Anyway, I think I already know why you're here this morning."

"You do?" Jo exclaimed.

Janet nodded rapidly. She opened a letter on her desk while she spoke. "It's about your job, right?"

"Right," Jo said uncertainly.

"I know exactly what's bothering you. It's that promotion I've been promising you."

Before Jo could respond, Janet jumped up and hurried to the door. "Okay, Jo. I'm going to tell you everything." Janet closed her office door securely. "I don't want anyone else to hear this conversation. Everything I tell you is strictly confidential." Janet pointed her finger towards Jo, waiting for confirmation that Jo understood the importance of her last statement.

Jo nodded dumbly. She hadn't the vaguest idea what Janet was going to say.

"Okay, Jo. For the past two months, I've been negotiating with Dorington Press." Janet walked across the room and sat down behind her desk. "Dorington Press has offered me a position as publisher of my own imprint."

"You're leaving Harris House?" Jo breathed, astonished.

"Yes, in all probability. I'm negotiating the fine points of my contract, but it looks as though we're pretty close to closing the deal. I wasn't going to resign until next month, so you understand this has got to be kept secret. You're the only one here who knows."

"I won't breathe a word to anyone," Jo said earnestly.

"I know you won't, dear. That's one of the reasons I'm telling you. But the real reason is to let you know that I've been thinking about your place in all of this. I haven't forgotten my promise to get you a promotion. I've been negotiating on your behalf as part of my deal with Dorington."

"I don't understand," Jo said.

"Well, Dorington has agreed to let me bring you with me when I move over there. You'll have the title of editor and your salary will be approximately doubled."

"You're kidding," Jo said, sitting upright in her chair.

"No, I'm not kidding," Janet laughed. "Isn't it great? You won't have to go through editorial assistant and then assistant editor. Jo, this is really a once-in-a-lifetime opportunity.

"But you certainly deserve it. I've never seen anyone learn as quickly or work as hard as you have. You handled the situation with Misha like a professional editor, and I'm going to see that you get the title and the salary to match the job you've done."

Jo was filled with pride and a sense of accomplishment that was stronger than anything she'd ever experienced. "Oh, Janet, thank you so much," she said humbly. "I'm so grateful. Really, I don't know what to say."

"Say nothing," Janet joked, reaching for her phone. Both extensions were ringing simultaneously. "Remember, this is strictly between us." Janet answered one line and indicated with a wave of her hand that Jo should pick up the other extension on her coffee table.

As both of them spoke on their respective phones, someone knocked on Janet's door.

"Come in!" Janet yelled.

Dacey marched into Janet's office, slamming the door behind her. She eyed Jo with great animosity.

"Janet, the marketing department is waiting for you. They're holding up their meeting. They've called three times," Dacey whined.

"Right, right. Tell them I'm on my way," Janet said hurriedly as she returned to her phone call.

Dacey turned sharply on her heel and walked out of Janet's office.

Janet slammed down her phone. "Jo, take care of these calls for me until I get back from the meeting. Call Bill and tell him I'll meet him for lunch at 12:30 at The King Cole Room of the St. Regis." Janet was out the door before Jo could respond.

Alone in Janet's office, Jo sank slowly into the couch. She could barely comprehend what Janet had just told her. In all the excitement, Jo had failed to tell Janet that she wanted to quit her job.

Jo marveled at her good luck. In the publishing hierarchy, a secretary had to spend years working herself up, first to editorial assistant (really a glorified secretary with some minor copywriting responsibilities) and then to assistant editor, line-editing manuscripts acquired by an editor. Acquisition of new books was the sole province of editors, and it was the goal toward which every editorial secretary strived.

Rarely could this goal be reached in less than five years—if you were very lucky. Also, it usually involved changing publishing houses frequently. Dacey, for instance, was still an editorial assistant after four years and two different companies. Janet's remark that this was a "once-in-a-lifetime opportunity" couldn't have been more accurate.

Jo was so proud of herself; she simply had to tell someone. Because of her promise to Janet, she couldn't tell anyone in the office. On the spur of the moment, she decided to run home for lunch and break the exciting news to Roarke.

Riding the subway back to Carmine Street, Jo wondered if Roarke would mind putting off their wedding for a few months. Naturally, if Roarke decided to move permanently to Los Angeles, Jo would quit her job and follow him out west. But until he made a final decision, Jo might as well take advantage of Janet's offer. As she pondered the logic of the situation, she gained more and more confidence that Roarke would agree with her.

Jo flew up the stairs to Roarke's apartment. When no one answered the doorbell, Jo pulled out her key and let herself into his apartment.

Roarke was gone. Disappointment washed over Jo; she hadn't even considered the possibility he wouldn't be home. Why didn't I call here first? she wondered ruefully.

Then, on a hunch, Jo searched Roarke's desk, finally locating his calendar. She turned to today's date and was delighted to discover Roarke's notation: 12:30, Lin's Garden.

Lin's Garden was Roarke's favorite restaurant in Chinatown. He and Jo had eaten there many times in the past two months.

Feeling very clever about her amateur sleuthing, Jo raced out of the apartment and took a cab downtown.

Lin's Garden was a small restaurant situated on one of the many sidestreets in Chinatown. As Jo approached the door to the restaurant, she recognized Roarke sitting at a table near the front window. He was eating rice from a small bowl and talking animatedly to an older man with silver hair.

Roarke didn't spot Jo until she was practically on top of his table. His chopsticks paused in midair, and the look on his face was of pure shock.

"Jo!" he exclaimed loudly. "What on earth are you doing here?" He dropped his chopsticks as he stood up. The older man with him also rose.

"Oh, please, don't get up," Jo said to the elderly gentleman. She kissed Roarke on the cheek. "Murphy, I have wonderful news. It couldn't wait until tonight, so I ran home to talk to you but you weren't there." Jo sat down on a chair and motioned for the two men to be seated. "I confess. I checked your calendar. And here I am," she said with a self-satisfied smile.

The two men stared awkwardly at each other as if they weren't quite sure what to do about Jo's intrusion.

For a moment Jo felt a twinge of guilt. Perhaps she'd been too impulsive. But, no, when Roarke heard her news, he'd understand, she thought consolingly to herself.

Meanwhile, she couldn't help wondering why Roarke hadn't introduced his luncheon companion to her. Why did they both seem so embarrassed by her presence?

Roarke cleared his throat. "Um, Jo, this is rather unexpected," he said slowly. Then he shrugged helplessly at the older man. "I guess the jig's up," he joked. "Joanna Davenport, may I introduce Misha Rakovich?" he said.

Jo's head spun toward Misha. She tried to talk but the words wouldn't come.

Misha smiled charmingly as if he understood her confusion. There was a deep kindness in his dark blue eyes. With his distinguished graying hair, Misha was an extremely handsome man. "Please don't feel bad, Jo. Sooner or later we were bound to run into each other. And, actually, I'm very glad you showed up today. Murphy just told me the good news about your impending marriage. Let me be the first to congratulate you. I hope you and Murphy will be very happy."

Jo looked from Misha to Roarke and back again to Misha. She wanted to speak but she couldn't. For the past few months, she mentally practiced a list of things she wanted to say to Misha when they finally met. But she was so shocked by this chance encounter that all she could do was stare helplessly at Misha.

Roarke chuckled at the perplexed look on her face. He pushed his mug of beer across the table. "Take a sip of this, Jo," he advised.

Nodding her head in agreement, Jo took a long swallow of beer. "Thanks," she said before turning to Misha. Finally, she felt able to talk. "It's a pleasure to meet you, Mr. Rakovich," she said diffidently. "I'm sorry if I seem a little flustered but, frankly, I am."

Misha laughed warmly. "Quite understandable, Jo. I apologize for the nuisance my secrecy has caused you. I hope you'll forgive the idiosyncrasies of an old man." Misha patted Jo's hand kindly.

"Oh, please don't apologize, Mr. Rakovich."

"Very well, my dear. As long as you stop this 'mister' business. Please call me Misha."

Jo returned his smile and nodded. She was totally captivated by the charming writer.

"Actually, it's fortunate we met. I wanted to discuss your last memo," Misha continued.

"About adding a bibliography to your book? I wondered—"

"Whoa!" Roarke interrupted. "No editorial talk at this table. You and Misha can discuss the book at another time."

Misha shook his head up and down. "Murphy is entirely correct," he said. "Besides, since we know each other personally now, we can dispense with our memos. Perhaps you can come up to my loft tomorrow, and we'll try to solve all our editorial problems over coffee."

"Oh, I'd love that," Jo said enthusiastically.

"For heaven's sake, Jo," Roarke groaned impatiently. "Tell us your news."

"Oh, of course," Jo said, startled that she'd held back the story for so long. "But first, please, both of you *promise* me you won't breathe a word of this to *anyone* at Harris House," Jo elongated each word for emphasis.

Both men murmured in agreement. Roarke pulled his chair closer to the table in mock seriousness. "Jo, I'm going to strangle you if you don't spit it out already," he cried in frustration.

"Okay." Jo clapped her hands together. "Here it is. Janet is leaving Harris House."

"You're kidding," Roarke said, genuinely surprised.

Jo smiled at his response, so like her own in situations like this. She shook her head from side to side. "No, I am definitely not kidding. Janet's been offered a job at Dorington Press as Publisher of her own imprint *and* she wants to take me with her. As an *editor!*" Jo exclaimed. She still couldn't get over how lucky she was.

"That's marvelous news, Joanna. Congratulations, again," Misha said.

"Thank you, Misha," Jo replied, and then she turned to Roarke. He was smiling broadly.

"I'm very proud of you, darling. That's quite an achievement, and you should be very proud of yourself." He leaned across the table and kissed her forehead. "It's just too bad you'll have to turn her down." Roarke sighed sympathetically. "I'm sorry you'll miss this opportunity." He turned to Misha. "Isn't this always the case?" he said to him. "Two days ago Jo would have jumped at this opportunity."

Jo shifted uncomfortably in her chair. "What do you mean, Murphy?" she asked. Even though she knew exactly what he meant, she needed to stall for time so she could collect her thoughts.

A look of confusion settled on Roarke's face. "Jo, we're moving to Los Angeles in a few days. How can you take this new job?"

Jo swallowed hard. This wasn't going to be easy at all. She looked nervously at Misha and then at Roarke.

"Jo," Roarke continued when she didn't respond, "Didn't you tell Janet we were planning on getting married and moving to L.A.?"

She felt as if she were losing control of the conversation, and she was petrified that Roarke would be angry, but she had to answer him honestly. "Well, no, not exactly. I didn't get around to telling her in all the excitement." Jo's voice trailed off into a whisper. She hesitated to tell Roarke that she really wanted to take the job even if it meant postponing their plans.

For a moment, no one spoke and an unbearably tense

silence settled between the three of them at the table. Roarke was staring at Jo in utter confusion.

Finally, Misha moved his chair and it scraped across the floor, breaking the silence. "Perhaps I should leave you two alone," he offered. "If you'll excuse me . . ."

"No," Roarke said loudly. "Stay where you are, Misha." Then he grabbed Jo's hand.

"Jo, what about our plans? What do you expect me to do if you take this job?" He looked away from her for a moment. "Don't you want to marry me?" he asked quietly.

"Oh, Murphy, I love you. Of course I want to marry you," Jo replied urgently. "I was just hoping we could wait a few months.

"Look, why don't you go to L.A. and work for a month without me? If you decide to settle there permanently, I'll be out on the next plane. There's always the chance that you'll hate California and want to move back to New York. Then I'd have to start all over with another secretarial job. Murphy, this is a once-in-a-lifetime opportunity for me. Please understand how much I want this job." Jo desperately tried to be as reasonable as possible, hoping Roarke would realize her commitment to her career didn't affect her love for him.

"What I don't understand," he said between clenched teeth, "is why I'm not more important to you than some silly job."

Jo could feel her back stiffen in anger. She tried to remain calm. "It is not a silly job, Roarke. My work is as meaningful to me as your writing is to you," she said defiantly.

"Oh, come on, Jo. You're a secretary," he said, waving his hand in disgust.

"I'm about to be promoted to an editor," she yelled. "I've worked hard for this promotion." Then, embarrassed by her outburst, she lowered her voice to a whisper. "I thought you wanted me to be independent," she added, crossing her arms over her chest and frowning.

"Knock it off, Jo. You don't need to sell that independence garbage to me. I happen to know how dependent you really are."

"I am independent," she cried. "I've made it on my own in New York!"

"On your own?" he sneered. "How far would you have gotten without my help?"

"Maybe a lot further than I am now," she countered in anger.

Her remark infuriated him. "Without me, you'd be back in Falls Creek by now. You couldn't even find an apartment without my help."

"I pay hard-earned money for that apartment."

Roarke laughed roughly. "My last tenant paid six hundred a month for that apartment."

"*Your* tenant?" Jo stammered.

"Yes. I own the building, Jo. Why do you think your rent is so low?"

His remark astonished Jo. She had had no idea that Roarke owned the building on Carmine Street. She'd always assumed she was subleasing from the former tenant.

Jo stared dumbly at Roarke, her confidence and self-assurance vanished into thin air. If the apartment really cost $600 a month, then Roarke was actually paying two-thirds of Jo's rent. In reality, Jo was being kept by Roarke as if she were his mistress. The thought brought scalding tears of humiliation to her eyes, but she adamantly refused to cry in front of him. At that moment, she truly hated him for deceiving her.

Roarke seemed to know instantly that he'd gone too far. He shook his head as if he couldn't believe his own stupidity. He reached over and tried to take Jo's hand but she pulled away from him.

"Jo, I'm sorry. I didn't mean that to sound the way it did. I didn't realize what I was saying," he said, genuinely distraught.

Jo wanted to forgive him but she was so hurt that she couldn't allow herself to feel anything but outrage. She fought to maintain her self-control.

"I'll increase my rent payment next month," she said, stubbornly refusing to acknowledge his apology.

"Jo, that's not important. Forget about the rent," he implored her, his voice heavy with emotion.

"No," she said haughtily. "Janet promised to double my salary with this new job. I'll be able to pay you fair market value for your apartment," she said, clipping each word with precision.

"Then you're taking the job?" he asked quietly.

"Yes. Most definitely," she replied.

"Then there's nothing more for us to discuss." Roarke extracted a twenty-dollar bill from his wallet and threw it on the table. "Misha, I apologize for making you witness this domestic squabble."

Misha waved his hand, dismissing Roarke's apology. His dark blue eyes were filled with sadness.

Roarke stared at Jo for a moment as if he were about to speak but then, changing his mind, he turned and started towards the door.

Suddenly, Jo panicked at the thought that Roarke was

walking out of her life. "Murphy, wait," she called out, jumping up and running after him. "Please don't leave like this. Isn't there some way we can work this out?"

"Will you come to California with me?" he asked.

She looked deeply into his coal black eyes, searching for a glimmer of understanding. Frustration and confusion washed over her. "Murphy, can't we compromise?" she cried. "I'm only asking for a month or two."

Roarke sighed wearily. "A lot can happen in a month or two," he warned. "But, all right. If that's the way you want it, so be it.

"I'll leave for L.A. tonight. If you change your mind, you're welcome to join me. If not, we'll both take our chances." Then he turned and walked out of the restaurant.

10

From the moment Roarke walked out of the restaurant in Chinatown, Jo had fought the urge to run after him. Now she clung desperately to the belief that she had done the right thing; her career was important, and Roarke had no right to make her choose between her work and him. It just wasn't fair. If he could have both, why couldn't she?

But it was getting harder and harder for Jo to stick to her decision. Being right wasn't keeping her warm at night. In fact, most nights Jo cried herself to sleep, longing for Roarke's body next to hers. In two months he had not written to her or called her.

As far as Jo knew, Misha was the only person who had spoken to Roarke since he had left for L.A.

Misha kept Jo informed of Roarke's activities in California, and she was very grateful to him for his kindness and understanding. In the past few weeks, Jo and Misha had become close friends. They met frequently for lunch or dinner. Sometimes they worked on Misha's book; other times they simply talked for hours.

Today Jo was very anxious to see Misha; she hurried to his loft on Greene Street, racing up the stairs to the second floor. She smiled at his nameplate on the door: M. Reardon. Misha used this pseudonym on almost everything.

Misha pulled open his door as soon as Jo rang the bell.

"I heard your footsteps," he said, kissing her on the cheek. "Only a young girl could run up those damn steps," he laughed.

Jo smiled warmly. "How are you today?" she asked.

"Fine, fine," he replied, taking her coat and hanging it on a hook near the door. "I've finished my column for tomorrow and I'm free for the whole afternoon." Misha clapped his hands together eagerly. "Why don't I cook up a few omelettes for lunch?"

"I'm not too hungry today, but you go ahead and make yourself something to eat," she said.

Misha shook his head. "No, we both eat. I insist. You must eat, Joanna. You're as thin as a rail. How much weight have you lost in the past few weeks?"

"A little." Jo shrugged, smoothing down her skirt. Misha often criticized Jo's haphazard eating habits and, by now, she knew it was easier to eat than to argue with him. "All right." She smiled. "I'll join you for lunch."

"Good," Misha said as he turned to his refrigerator. He extracted a box of mushrooms and ran them under the water. "Here, you cut the mushrooms for me." He handed her a small cutting board and a knife.

Jo started slicing mushrooms. She felt compelled to find out if Roarke had called recently, but she was too shy to ask a direct question. "Anything new with you?" she asked demurely.

Misha turned to face her. His blue eyes glanced at her for a moment and then he looked away quickly. "I haven't heard from Roarke this week," he said softly as if he were reading her mind. "But don't you worry about him. He'll call in due time."

Jo shook her head helplessly. If only she could stop herself from asking about him. She wished she could put Roarke out of her mind but, in her heart, she knew that was impossible. Even three thousand miles away from her, Roarke was the focus of Jo's life.

Misha shook his head. "I wish I could erase the sadness from your face," he said compassionately. "That boy should be ashamed of himself. He has no right to treat you this way," Misha added angrily.

"Please don't get upset," Jo said softly.

"I'm not upset," Misha yelled. "I'm angry. Murphy is acting like a stubborn old goat."

"Misha," Jo whispered, "have I made a mistake by not going to Los Angeles with Roarke?" This was the first time Jo had vocalized the question that had haunted her for weeks.

Misha reached across the counter and touched Jo's hand sympathetically. "I can't answer your question, Jo. Only you know what is right for Joanna Davenport. But I do know you did what you felt had to be done. Right or wrong, you acted on your feelings. I've lived my whole life that way, Jo, and all I can tell you is that I've never regretted it."

Jo looked up at his kind face and smiled. "Thank you, Misha," she said.

"For what?" he asked, perplexed.

"Oh, for being such a good friend. I'm so grateful I have you to talk to," she said sincerely.

Misha patted her hand again and then he returned to his stove. "Anytime you need to talk, you call me," he said as he flipped the omelettes. He looked over his shoulder at Jo. "I'm always here for you," he added.

Unable to reply to his kind words, Jo nodded her head in appreciation.

A few minutes later, Misha handed Jo a plate filled with an omelette and sliced tomatoes. He sat down next to her at the counter.

"Tell me about your column for tomorrow," Jo said as she buttered her roll.

The phone rang before Misha could answer Jo. He jumped off the stool and hurried to his desk.

"Hello," he said.

"Yes, operator, this is M. Reardon speaking," Misha said.

Jo turned to smile at Misha; it always amused her to hear him use his other name.

Misha was frowning and he turned his head to avoid Jo's gaze.

Jo's forehead wrinkled in confusion but, a moment later, she understood Misha's embarrassment.

"Hello, Murphy," Misha said stiffly. "How are you?"

Jo spun around in her chair, hiding her face from Misha. She was certain her eyes revealed her sudden panic. She tried to sip her coffee, but her hand was shaking too much to hold the cup.

"No, nothing's wrong, Murphy," Misha continued, his

voice softening a little. "In fact, I was just talking about you."

Misha paused for a moment. "Never mind what I was saying. It's none of your business. How are things in L.A.?"

"Oh, I see. Yes, I'll be happy to do it. Just give me the information."

Jo could hear Misha fumbling through his desk drawer. "Okay, I found a pencil," he said.

The loft seemed deathly quiet to Jo. The only sound she heard was Misha's pencil scratching across a piece of paper.

"Yes, I've got it. Flight 102, American Airlines, three forty-five, Kennedy Airport."

Another short pause.

"No, no problem at all."

"Okay, I'll see you then. So long." Misha hung up the phone. He sat at his desk for a few moments before walking back to the counter.

Meanwhile, Jo's heart was pounding in her chest. Her eyes stared straight ahead; she felt as if she couldn't move.

Misha slid onto the stool next to Jo. "That was Roarke," he said casually.

"So I gathered," Jo said as calmly as possible. "What did he want?" she asked. With her fork, Jo pushed a mushroom across her plate. Her appetite had completely vanished.

Misha bit into a roll. "He needs a ride home from the airport tomorrow. He asked me to pick him up at Kennedy."

"Is he home for good or just to pick up his belongings?"

Misha shrugged. "He didn't say. He was calling from a meeting, so he didn't have much time to talk."

Jo bit her lower lip.

Suddenly, Misha snapped his fingers. "Oh, nuts," he exclaimed. "I have a meeting tomorrow afternoon. I'd forgotten all about it."

Misha jumped off the stool and rushed to his desk. "Yes. There it is," he said, pointing to his desk calendar. "Three o'clock, John Stern's office."

Jo walked over to Misha, but he snapped his calendar shut before she could verify the notation.

Misha pulled a set of keys out of his pocket. "I have an idea," he said, handing her the keys. "You take my car and meet Murphy at the airport."

Jo stared at Misha in disbelief. "Me?" she said in amazement.

"Why not?" Misha laughed. "Here, take the keys and this piece of paper." He pressed both objects into Jo's hand. "The flight number is on that scrap of paper.

"My car is parked in the open lot on the corner of Greene Street. I'll call the garage and clear it with them," he said.

"Oh, Misha, I can't do this," Jo said despondently. "How can I just show up at the airport? I'd be making a fool of myself."

"Maybe so, my dear." Misha grinned. "But people in love always make fools of themselves. It's the best part about love; you don't have to worry about appearing foolish."

When she didn't respond to his remark, he shrugged. "But, I won't force you to do anything that doesn't feel right. If you don't want to meet Roarke, we'll let him find his own transportation home." Misha reached for the keys in Jo's hand.

She snapped her hand away from him. "No," she cried. "I'll do it." She leaned over and kissed Misha on the cheek. "Thank you, Misha," she murmured.

He returned her kiss. "Anytime, my dear," he said. Then, walking back to the counter, he picked up their luncheon plates and carried them over to the sink.

Jo dropped the keys and the piece of paper in her purse. "Misha, if you don't mind, I think I'll be going now. I'd better get back to the office and do a little work so I can leave early tomorrow." Jo hurried to the door and grabbed her coat.

"Jo," Misha called out suddenly.

"Um?" she said absentmindedly. She was already thinking about seeing Roarke tomorrow.

"Just one question: You do know how to drive a car, don't you?" he asked with an embarrassed grin.

Laughing, Jo nodded her head. "If I didn't, I'd learn by tomorrow," she joked as she closed the door behind her.

Jo could hear Misha's laughter echoing in the halls as she raced down the stairs.

At the office the next afternoon, Jo told Janet she was leaving for the day, claiming that she had "personal business to attend to." Somewhat reluctantly, Janet agreed to Jo's request.

Jo raced out of the office to Misha's garage downtown. The attendant at the parking lot seemed to be expecting her. In a few minutes, Jo was behind the wheel of Misha's gray Datsun, easing the sportscar into afternoon traffic.

Several road signs on the expressway directed Jo to the airport and, pulling into a parking space near the American Airlines terminal, she turned off the car's engine and hurried into the crowded airport. After what seemed like hours, she finally heard the announcement over the loudspeaker: "American Airlines Flight 102 from Los Angeles is now arriving at Gate 23."

Naturally, Gate 23 was clear across the terminal. Jo felt as if she had walked five miles by the time she arrived at the proper gate.

Peering out the window, Jo saw the huge 747 airplane taxi into position on the runway.

The first people to emerge from the plane were business types, men and women who carried overstuffed briefcases and raced down the runway. Few of them noticed the people standing around. Obviously, they were not expecting to be met at the terminal.

Jo smoothed down her coat. Then, just when she thought Roarke must have missed the flight, she saw the top of his head. As always, Roarke towered above the crowd.

His face was handsomely tanned. He looked well-rested and cheerful as he sauntered off the plane. In his hand, he carried his familiar leather flight bag.

Jo's heart started to hammer in her chest, and she could feel her throat go dry. All she wanted to do was race across the waiting room and throw herself into Roarke's arms.

Roarke scanned the faces of the people standing around the immediate area. Not expecting to see Jo, his eyes passed by her quickly. Then his head snapped around and he stopped walking for a second, so suddenly that a blonde woman behind him crashed into Roarke's back.

Roarke turned and spoke to the woman.

Jo couldn't hear what he said to her, but the blonde

173

waved her hand and smiled flirtatiously at him. For a moment Jo lost sight of him.

But when she turned around again, Roarke was standing directly in front of her.

For a moment, neither of them seemed able to speak. They stood staring into each other's eyes.

Jo reacted first. "Welcome home, Roarke," she said shyly.

He nodded slowly. "What happened to Misha?" he asked, looking around the airport lounge.

His tone of voice was so unemotional that all thoughts of rushing into his arms vanished from Jo's mind. Had she made a mistake by coming to meet him?

Self-consciously she backed away from Roarke. "Misha couldn't make it. He had a meeting, so he asked me to pick you up." She lowered her eyes.

"I see. Well, it was very nice of you to drive all this way," he said.

"Oh, it was no problem," Jo replied with a shrug.

Roarke shifted his flight bag from one hand to the other. "I'd better go pick up my luggage," he said. "It's down this ramp." Avoiding each other's eyes, Jo and Murphy walked down the corridor.

Neither of them spoke as they walked. Roarke's forehead was furrowed, and he seemed to concentrate all his energy on staring straight ahead.

Jo felt as though Roarke was miles away from her. As they waited for the luggage to come down the ramp, the silence between them grew more and more nerve-racking. Jo made an attempt at some small talk, but Roarke answered every one of her questions curtly. Jo's hands were trembling from the effort of trying to remain calm.

In a few minutes, Roarke retrieved his suitcase from the ramp, and they hurried out of the terminal.

At the car, he tossed his luggage in the backseat. "Do you want me to drive?" he asked.

Grateful that she wouldn't have to concentrate on driving, Jo handed him the keys. Roarke turned on the ignition. "So, how'd you like Los Angeles?" she asked to break the silence.

Roarke eased Misha's car out of the parking space. "Great, just great. California is a very seductive place to live." His voice was strangely unenthusiastic considering his careful choice of words.

"Seductive?" Jo asked, wondering if she had heard him correctly.

Roarke nodded. "Yes, seductive. Every morning you wake up and the sun is shining. The weather is so beautiful all the time that you never feel like working. Most days you seem to wind up sitting by the pool instead of the typewriter."

Jo fidgeted with her purse. "It must be difficult to write if you're submerged under water all day," Jo said sarcastically. Then she quickly changed her tone of voice. "How's the screenplay coming along?" she asked.

"Very slowly," he replied.

"I'm sorry to hear that. What's the problem?"

"Don't know," he said. "But I did have an awful lot of distractions in L.A."

Jo's heart sank. She stared thoughtfully out of her window, watching the houses pass by as the car sped down the expressway.

"So, Misha tells me you're still at Harris House," Roarke commented, interrupting Jo's thoughts.

"Yes," she said, nodding her head.

Roarke took his eyes off the road for a moment to glance at Jo. "What happened?" he asked, showing real interest in Jo for the first time that afternoon.

"When Janet tried to resign, Mr. Harris insisted that she change her mind," Jo said, reacting happily to Roarke's attention. "Mr. Harris offered Janet the same deal she'd gotten from Dorington, plus a larger percentage of the profits." Jo shrugged. "So Janet decided to stay."

"And what about you?"

"I'm now Editor of Tarlin Books, a division of Harris House. I have my own secretary, I'm publishing my first novel next season, and I'm sending over a hundred dollars a month to my mother," Jo said proudly.

Roarke smiled warmly at Jo. He stopped the car at the tollbooth by the Midtown Tunnel. "That's very impressive, Jo. You've come a long way in a short time. Your mother must be very proud of you," he said. "And you've all the right in the world to be proud of yourself."

His voice was very sincere, and Jo felt a flicker of hope that Roarke had come to understand the importance of her career. Perhaps it wasn't too late to patch things up between them.

Roarke paid the toll and edged the car into the tunnel.

"We're very excited about our first list at Tarlin Books," Jo continued talking about her job. "By staying with Harris House, Janet was able to keep her authors; that's one of the reasons she didn't leave. So, our first list consists of two major works: *The Finlandia Affair* and *In My Opinion: A Collection of Essays by Misha Rakovich.*"

Roarke grinned. "Sounds a bit chauvinistic to me. Don't you publish women authors?"

"Next season," Jo assured him. "My new novel is by a woman."

"Terrific!" Roarke exclaimed. "I'm honored to be the first Tarlin Book on the market."

Roarke drove out of the Midtown Tunnel and steered the car down Second Avenue. He found a parking space on their block, and Jo helped him carry everything into the house.

"How about coffee?" Jo asked, hoping to spend more time with him.

"Um, I think a glass of wine would be better," he said as he removed his coat, hanging it on the hook by the door. Then he reached for Jo's coat.

Their hands touched briefly, and they both looked up at the same time.

For a moment, they stood staring at each other. Roarke raised one hand and lightly touched Jo's cheek. It was almost as if he had to touch her in order to confirm her presence in the room. She could feel the familiar primitive passion he always aroused in her, and she was startled by the powerful sensation. In two months, she had almost forgotten how strongly she was attracted to him.

He leaned over and lightly kissed her cheek. Then, as if embarrassed, he turned and hurried into the kitchen.

He returned to the living room with an opened bottle of wine and glasses. "You pour," he said. "I have to call my answering service."

Roarke disappeared into the bedroom while Jo splashed wine into the glasses. He was gone for a long time but he seemed very excited when he returned to the living room.

"Okay," he said, clapping his hands together once.

"The plans for tonight are all set." He grabbed a glass of wine and took a long swallow.

"Wear something dressy, and you only have a half hour so you'd better hurry."

"What are you talking about?" Jo said, utterly confused.

"I've made arrangements for tonight."

"What arrangements?" Jo asked.

"Never mind. You'll find out soon enough," he said mysteriously.

Jo shrugged, not knowing quite how to take his remark. "I'll just go get ready," she said uncertainly, placing her wineglass on the coffee table and walking toward the door.

"Right," he replied, rushing into his bedroom.

Jo ran upstairs to her apartment. Quickly undressing, she took a hot shower.

While she hurriedly dressed for the evening, Jo tried to make sense of her meeting with Roarke.

She really had no idea how Roarke felt about California; he'd barely mentioned L.A., much less his plans for the future. Did he want to live permanently in California? And what, in heaven's name, were his mysterious plans for this evening?

As she brushed her honey-blond hair, Jo relived the sensation of Roarke's tender kiss when they had first entered his apartment. Despite her anxieties about the future, her attraction for him was certainly as powerful as ever. She sighed loudly. Tonight she would be with him, and that was all that really mattered.

Jo slipped into her black, sling-back pumps. Although she had to wear her lilac dress, the high heels and her jet-beaded evening purse made the outfit a touch more dressy.

She rushed down the stairs to Roarke's apartment. His door was open and she let herself into the apartment.

"It's me," Jo called out.

"Be right with you," Roarke said. In a few minutes he walked out of the bedroom and glanced quickly at his watch. "We'd better hurry," he said.

Grabbing Jo's hand, Roarke pulled her out of the apartment, and they rushed down the street.

They got a cab on the corner, and Roarke asked the driver to take them to Central Park South. Roarke hummed cheerfully as the taxi sped uptown.

When they arrived at the Park, they got out of the cab and Roarke put his arm around Jo's shoulders. Jo didn't know where they were going, but at the moment she didn't care. She was with Roarke and, for the first time in two months, she felt truly alive again.

They walked over to one of the horse-drawn carriages waiting by the entrance to the park.

"Evening, sir," said the top-hatted driver. "Care for a ride in my carriage this evening?"

"You bet!" Roarke exclaimed. "We want the grand tour." Roarke helped Jo climb into the buggy. "Drive us to Times Square," he said.

"Right you are, sir!" the driver said with a snap of his head. "It's a lovely night for a ride."

With a flick of the reins, the huge gray mare started off at an easy pace. The horse's hooves clacked over the pavement as they rode down Fifth Avenue.

Roarke hugged Jo closely to his chest. She laid her head against his shoulder and relaxed into his arms.

For a long time they didn't speak. In a way, it was as if they both had to privately gather their thoughts.

Roarke broke the silence first. "I don't know how I survived the past two months, Jo," he said softly. He looked away for a moment. "I've missed you so much," he whispered.

Jo stared down at her lap. She wished they could just forget the past two months; she longed to put the past behind them. But she couldn't let it go at this brief remark. She needed to settle her doubts and fears once and for all. She had to find out why he'd left her in limbo for such a long time. Taking a deep breath, she looked up into his coal black eyes. "Why didn't you write or call me? It's been such a long time," she said, her voice cracking slightly.

He sighed. "I don't know why. Jo, I just couldn't. I guess I had to sort things out by myself. I was so angry when I left New York. I couldn't forgive you for not coming with me."

Scalding tears burned Jo's eyes. "Oh, Murphy, don't you understand that my decision to stay here had nothing to do with the way I felt about you?" she cried.

He nodded his head slowly. "I know that now, but it took me a long time to get past my anger. I felt betrayed by your loyalty to Janet. I thought your job meant more to you than I did." He grimaced as if he couldn't believe his own behavior. "Everything was all mixed up in my mind. Look, Jo, you were absolutely right to stay in New York. It was ridiculous and small-minded of me to expect you to jeopardize your career on one of my silly whims."

"Do you really believe that now?" she asked.

"Yes, yes I do," he said emphatically, tightly holding her hand. "Jo, I met a lot of women in California. One night I was at a party in Beverly Hills; I'd had more than my share of champagne, and I met this absolutely gorgeous Hollywood starlet."

Jo's throat constricted with jealousy. She wasn't at all sure she wanted to hear Roarke's story.

"Anyway," he continued, "we got to talking, and I suddenly realized I was having the same conversation with this woman that I'd had with a dozen other young starlets. We discussed the people at that particular party, the latest Hollywood gossip, and New York City as the crime capital of the world." He shook his head disgustedly. "I was bored to tears."

"What did you do?" Jo asked, more concerned about how the "starlet" felt than Roarke's boredom.

"I got in my rented car, drove home, and booked the next flight to New York. I felt I would go absolutely crazy if I didn't see you immediately."

Jo felt a warm security bubbling up inside her, and it gave her the courage to ask an even more important question—one that had plagued her ever since their first night together.

"Roarke, there's one more question I have to ask you," Jo said slowly. "I've been wanting to ask this question for a long time."

"Um," he murmured, caressing her cheek.

She cleared her throat softly. "Why me?" she asked. Her heart was pounding so loudly in her chest that she was certain Roarke could hear it beating.

He laughed incredulously. "Are you serious?"

"Of course I'm serious." She gently pushed him away from her. "Murphy, you're a very famous writer. You must meet all kinds of beautiful women. Even Hollywood starlets. I'm sure you could have your pick of them. And yet, from the very first, you seemed to want me.

"I mean, I know I'm okay. My hips are a little lumpy but, other than that, my looks are passable." When she looked up she noticed he was staring intently at her, and she lost some of her courage to continue. "I just don't understand why you picked me . . ." Her voice trailed off into a whisper.

"Oh, my darling," he said slowly. "Don't you know how special you are?" His eyes were rounded in amazement. "I'm surprised you don't know this, but you're an extremely attractive woman; any man would desire you. And, as for this man"—Roarke pointed to his chest—"I haven't felt so strongly attracted to a woman in years. Jo, for the past few years, I've been consumed by work. I told myself I just didn't have the time for a social life. But, in my heart, I knew that if the right woman came along, I'd have plenty of time. Before I published my first book, I was one of those starving artists that women loved to mother. After my books were published and I became a minor celebrity, women wanted to show me off at dinner parties as if I were some kind of trophy." He shrugged. "Neither situation was particularly attractive and, after a while, I gave up altogether. I decided that a comfortable bachelorhood was my lot in life, so I threw myself into work. And then I ran into you."

"Quite literally," Jo giggled, remembering their first encounter.

He nodded. "Something about you was different. Maybe it was your defiance or your stubbornness when you refused to smile at me," he continued, also remembering that first day they met in the office. "I don't know. All I do know is that I felt something very powerful and, suddenly, I felt alive for the first time in years. I had to see you again."

His lips curved into a happy grin. "Remember our second meeting when I found you in Janet's office?"

Jo nodded. "You came back to get your wallet."

"Not really." He chuckled. "I have a confession. I came back to see you again. All the way out of the office and down Sixth Avenue I kept thinking about you. I couldn't get you out of my mind. I simply had to find out who you were.

"So I went back to the office, and the receptionist told me you were with Janet. I stormed into Janet's office to see you again."

"But your wallet . . ." Jo stammered.

He laughed again. "My wallet was in my pocket until I turned around. Luckily, you didn't seem to notice, but Janet did. I was awfully embarrassed that Janet caught me acting like a teenager, but I needed some excuse to barge into her office and meet you."

Jo smiled from ear to ear. She was so enthralled by his confession that all her insecurity seemed to vanish. "Oh, Murphy," she said, tears welling up in her eyes. "I don't know what to say." She took his hand and held it to her cheek.

He gently kissed her earlobe. "Just say you'll forgive me for being such a fool these past two months," he whispered.

"Only if you'll forgive me," she said, her voice choked with emotion.

"Oh, Joanna, my darling," he moaned. His warm lips covered her mouth with tiny kisses and Jo felt as though her heart would explode with excitement.

Then, suddenly, Roarke released her and leaned

forward. "We'll get off here," he said urgently to the driver of the carriage.

"In the middle of Times Square?" the driver asked.

"Yes," Roarke said.

The carriage came to a stop and Roarke jumped out. Holding Jo by her waist, he lifted her out of the carriage.

Jo was totally confused by Roarke's sudden decision to get out of the carriage. It had been so lovely riding down the streets of the city, why did he want to stop here? Times Square was noisy and jammed with people.

"Isn't that the greatest billboard in the world?" Roarke exclaimed, pointing to the electric sign that dominated Times Square.

In total confusion, Jo looked up at the billboard. A thousand different colored lightbulbs flashed out the message: *Listen to WBGH, the best in country music.* "Yes, it's very nice," Jo said, perplexed.

"Murphy, could you please explain why we've stopped here?" Jo said, bewildered.

Roarke paid the driver, and then he glanced at his watch. "I wanted to show you something," he said.

"Okay." She shrugged. "What?"

"Just keep watching over there." He pointed to the billboard.

Jo sighed as she crossed her arms over her chest. They waited in silence for a few minutes. "Roarke, this is crazy," Jo said, pulling her coat collar tighter around her neck. "It's freezing here; can't we go someplace warm and sit down . . . ?"

A huge grin spread across Roarke's mouth. He gently

held Jo's shoulders and twisted her around so she stood facing the billboard.

Jo's hand flew to her mouth.

The billboard read: *Joanna Davenport!*

She turned to Roarke, her mouth frozen in surprise. Then she spun around again.

The lights were flashing, forming a new message: *Will you Marry Me?*

The flashing lights mesmerized her. She couldn't take her eyes off the sign as the letters rearranged themselves.

A cry escaped Jo's lips as she read the final message: *I Love You. Roarke.*

Her vision blurred with tears as the sign changed into an ad for another radio station.

Roarke grinned sheepishly at her. "I could only afford ten seconds," he said. "Or else I would have added a promise. I'll never again ask you to choose between your career and me, Jo."

Jo was too overcome with emotion to speak at the moment.

"Jo, my darling," Roarke continued. "All I want is you. I don't want to live in California; I'm no damned good at all that Hollywood glamor. I don't care how much money they offer me. I hate writing screenplays. We can manage on a writer's income, Jo."

"And an editor's salary," Jo added with a smile.

He held her shoulders tightly. "Then you'll marry me?" he asked softly.

"Of course I will, my love."

Roarke swept Jo into his arms. They kissed each other hungrily.

Several people, passing them on the crowded street, stopped to stare at their passionate embrace. Someone in the crowd whistled softly. But neither Jo nor Roarke noticed that they were attracting attention.

In the middle of New York's busiest intersection, Broadway and Times Square, Joanna Davenport and Murphy Roarke sealed with a kiss the most intimate pledge known to lovers: they vowed eternal devotion to each other. Nothing would ever separate them again.

Coming Next Month

Renaissance Man by Stephanie James

Rare book dealer Alina Corey decided to live like the heroine of her favorite Renaissance book. It worked . . . until Jared Troy, a Renaissance scholar, challenged her to leave her storybook world and face a passion as grand as her dreams!

September Morning by Diana Palmer

Blake Hamilton was determined to control Kathryn but keep his heart free. She tried to rebel in the arms of another man, until a furious Blake promised to teach her a lesson she would never forget—plunging them both into a fiery passion.

On Wings Of Night by Constance Conrad

In one wild night of love Cara Williams had abandoned herself to publisher Quinn Alexander. Now she was faced with the prospect of working for him and wondered if she could deny the fulfillment she found in his arms.

Silhouette Desire

Coming Next Month

Passionate Journey by Thea Lovan

In the silver Moroccan moonlight Phillipa Bentley was swept away by passion for Raoul Mendoub, who claimed her sweetness with his plundering kisses. She tried to rebel but found this dark, enchanted prince had bewitched her soul.

Enchanted Desert by Suzanne Michelle

Jana Fleming had inherited Santa Fe's most famous gallery, but she hadn't expected artist Fletcher Logan to be part of her legacy as well! Overwhelmed by his touch, Jana knew Fletcher was her fate and her future.

Past Forgetting by Pamela Lind

Amanda Adams, prim and proper film goddess, had finally met her match in Alex Wojyclas, the principal backer of her latest film. In his arms her icy reserve melted and she soon found herself giving in to passion's implacable demands.

YOU'LL BE SWEPT AWAY
WITH SILHOUETTE DESIRE

$1.75 each

1 ☐ CORPORATE AFFAIR
Stephanie James

2 ☐ LOVE'S SILVER WEB
Nicole Monet

3 ☐ WISE FOLLY
Rita Clay

4 ☐ KISS AND TELL
Suzanne Carey

5 ☐ WHEN LAST WE LOVED
Judith Baker

6 ☐ A FRENCHMAN'S KISS
Kathryn Mallory

7 ☐ NOT EVEN FOR LOVE
Erin St. Claire

8 ☐ MAKE NO PROMISES
Sherry Dee

9 ☐ MOMENT IN TIME
Suzanne Simms

10 ☐ WHENEVER I LOVE YOU
Alana Smith

$1.95 each

11 ☐ VELVET TOUCH
Stephanie James

12 ☐ THE COWBOY AND THE
LADY Diana Palmer

13 ☐ COME BACK, MY LOVE
Pamela Wallace

14 ☐ BLANKET OF STARS
Lorraine Valley

15 ☐ SWEET BONDAGE
Dorothy Vernon

16 ☐ DREAM COME TRUE
Ann Major

17 ☐ OF PASSION BORN
Suzanne Simms

18 ☐ SECOND HARVEST
Erin Ross

19 ☐ LOVER IN PURSUIT
Stephanie James

20 ☐ KING OF DIAMONDS
Penny Allison

21 ☐ LOVE IN THE CHINA SEA
Judith Baker

22 ☐ BITTERSWEET IN BERN
Cheryl Durant

23 ☐ CONSTANT STRANGER
Linda Sunshine

24 ☐ SHARED MOMENTS
Mary Lynn Baxter

SILHOUETTE DESIRE, Department SD/6
1230 Avenue of the Americas
New York, NY 10020

Please send me the books I have checked above. I am enclosing $_____
(please add 50¢ to cover postage and handling. NYS and NYC residents
please add appropriate sales tax). Send check or money order—no cash or
C.O.D.'s please. Allow six weeks for delivery.

NAME _____

ADDRESS _____

CITY _____ STATE/ZIP _____

Silhouette Desire
Now Available

Lover In Pursuit by Stephanie James

Renya MacKenzie vowed she'd never again
succumb to Trevor Langdon's promise of passion. But
she soon found herself willing to submit to the
love she so desperately wanted.

King Of Diamonds by Penny Allison

Jo Ryan, sports reporter, made her first career
hit at Carney Gallagher's expense. Gallagher vowed
to even the score . . . but Jo never imagined that
passion would be the weapon of his choice.

Love In The China Sea by Judith Baker

From the moment Anne Hunter met Kai
Shanpei she was lost in his spell. The mysterious
Eurasian tycoon lifted her from reality and
transported her to the realm of fantasy.

Bittersweet In Bern by Cheryl Durant

Working in Switzerland with the famed author
Peter Imhof was a dream come true for Gabi. And
as the days passed she dared to dream anew—a dream
that could only be fulfilled in Peter's arms.

Constant Stranger by Linda Sunshine

Roarke had helped Joanna with her career
every step of the way: now could she give up the job
of a lifetime for a stormy, perilous love?

Shared Moments by Mary Lynn Baxter

He was the devil in disguise and Courtney
Roberts tried to keep Kace at arm's length. But
he took possession of her and drove her to
the heights of rapture.

Enjoy your own special time with Silhouette Romances.

Send for 6 books today— one is yours <u>free</u>!

Silhouette Romances take you into a special world of thrilling drama, tender passion, and romantic love. These are enthralling stories from your favorite romance authors—tales of fascinating men and women, set in exotic locations all over the world.

Convenient free home delivery. We'll send you six exciting Silhouette Romances to look over for 15 days. If you enjoy them as much as we think you will, pay the invoice enclosed with your trial shipment. **One book is yours free to keep.** Silhouette Romances are delivered right to your door with never a charge for postage or handling. There's no minimum number of books to buy, and you may cancel at any time.

Silhouette ❤ *Romances*